The Jazzman's Trumpet

A Kit Mystery

by Elizabeth Cody Kimmel

✖ American Girl®

Published by American Girl Publishing
Copyright © 2015 American Girl

Questions or comments? Call 1-800-845-0005,
visit **americangirl.com**, or write to Customer Service,
American Girl, 8400 Fairway Place, Middleton, WI 53562.

Printed in China
15 16 17 18 19 20 21 LEO 10 9 8 7 6 5 4 3 2 1

The following individuals and organizations have given permission
to use images incorporated into the cover design: theater interior, Narcis
Parfenti/Shutterstock.com; jazz band, © Jeffrey Jessop/fotoLibra;
background pattern on back cover, © kirstypargeter/Crestock.

Cover image by Juliana Kolesova

Cataloging-in-Publication Data available from the Library of Congress

For my Poet, TR,
who speaks Jazz.

Beforever™

The adventurous characters you'll meet in
the BeForever books will spark your curiosity
about the past, inspire you to find your voice
in the present, and excite you about your future.
You'll make friends with these girls as you share
their fun and their challenges. Like you, they are
bright and brave, imaginative and energetic,
creative and kind. Just as you are, they are
discovering what really matters: Helping others.
Being a true friend. Protecting the earth.
Standing up for what's right. Read their stories,
explore their worlds, join their adventures.
Your friendship with them will BeForever.

TABLE *of* CONTENTS

chapter 1
The Pitch

KIT KITTREDGE LEANED in so close
to the radio her nose was practically touching the
volume dial. As soon as she heard the final notes of
a popular jazz tune, she squeezed her father's hand.
"This is it!" she squealed. "Do you think I'll win?"

Dad gave her a hopeful look and put his finger
to his lips to signal quiet as the announcer's voice
came on the radio.

"And now, ladies and gentlemen, the moment
you've all been waiting for. The King Jazz Hour will
announce the winner of the free concert tickets . . .
right after a word from our sponsor: Sudso Soap.
When stains must go, use Sudso!"

When Kit heard the tinny sounds of the commercial begin, she let out a cry of exasperation.

"Another commercial? Oh, I'm on pins and needles!" Kit exclaimed.

"You mustn't be too disappointed if you don't win," Dad told her. "Hundreds and hundreds of people entered the contest."

"I know," Kit said, trying not to fidget with impatience. "I just want the waiting to be over."

As if on cue, the commercial ended, and the announcer's voice returned.

"Okay, folks, sorry to keep you on the edge of your seats. We've picked a postcard at random from a lucky listener who will win two front-row tickets to Swingin' Slim Simpson's exclusive one-night show at the Burns Theater right here in Cincinnati this Saturday night. The show is completely sold out, folks, and these are the very last two tickets. So without further ado, the name of our winning listener is ... Miss Kit Kittredge! You can pick up your tickets at the box office at any time. Thanks for listening, folks!"

Kit gasped as Dad let out something between a whoop and a laugh. "Golly, Kit!" he exclaimed.

Kit laughed, her disbelief turning to excitement. "I really won!"

"You really did," Dad said, chuckling and shaking his head in amazement as he switched the radio off. "Swingin' Slim Simpson is going to be the next huge jazz sensation, I'm sure of it."

Kit loved listening to the King Jazz Hour every Monday evening with her father. It was so much fun hearing him talk about the musicians and bandleaders, with wonderful-sounding names like Duke Ellington, Jelly Roll Morton, and Fats Waller. Kit knew very little about jazz, but she loved learning.

"Say, Kit," said Dad, "this would make a terrific article for the *Cincinnati Register*. The great Swingin' Slim comes to town. One night only!"

Kit's already pounding heart skipped a beat.

"Oh, it would," Kit agreed, her mind already

racing with possibilities. "But I expect Mr. Gibson has already asked one of his reporters to cover the show."

Dad smiled. "And if he hasn't? You're one of Mr. Gibson's reporters too, Kit."

Kit's cheeks warmed with pride. "Only for the children's section. This is a grown-up concert."

"Well, you ought to ask him," Dad pressed. "You just won front-row seats to the hottest show in town. How often does someone like Swingin' Slim perform at the Burns Theater? He's been hitting the most famous jazz clubs on this tour— the Savoy, the Cotton Club. Mr. Gibson might not realize what a big deal this concert is for our town. What an honor it is."

Kit nodded seriously. "I hadn't thought of it that way," she said. "You're right, Dad. I *will* go and talk to Mr. Gibson about it. I'll pitch him the story. But when a reporter makes a pitch to an editor, she's got to really do her homework first. Hang on one second—I'll be right back."

Kit dashed out of the living room and up two flights of stairs to her attic bedroom. Her reporter's notebook was right where she'd left it on the desk in the corner. Kit grabbed the book and a freshly sharpened pencil and clattered back down the staircase, taking the last steps two at a time. When she skidded back into the living room, trying to catch her breath, Dad shook his head with amusement.

"I like your enthusiasm, kid," he said with an affectionate smile. "So tell me how I can help you do your homework for this pitch."

Kit opened her notebook to a new page and sat down next to Dad. "Tell me everything you know about Swingin' Slim Simpson."

Dad laughed. "I'll do my best. Well, as most local jazz fans know, Slim was born here," Dad told Kit. "He lived in my old neighborhood, as a matter of fact. We went to the same high school, but he was three years younger than me so I never much noticed him. I sure was proud, though, when he started making a name for himself. Our very own Cincinnati star. Maybe that has something to do with why he decided to include the Burns Theater on his tour."

"Could be," Kit remarked, writing as quickly as she could.

"At some point I remember hearing that Slim left Cincinnati. I suppose if you want to make a name for yourself as a trumpet player, you've got to go where the music is. And at the time, that pretty much meant New York, Kansas City, or Chicago. Slim picked Chicago."

"Chicago. Chi-ca-go," Kit repeated, partly because she was working out how to spell it, and partly to buy herself a little time as she tried to write down everything Dad told her.

"Right," Dad said. "Everyone who was anyone in jazz played in Chicago. When a hot new player showed up, the word probably spread fast. Slim was on his way up. Who knows—maybe he was already dreaming of putting together his own band."

"So Swingin' Slim always wanted his own band?" Kit asked.

"Oh, I have no idea," Dad replied. "If you really want to know, you'll have to ask him."

Kit's pencil froze mid-word. "An interview with Swingin' Slim Simpson?"

"Why not?" Dad said. "If Mr. Gibson does let you cover the story, you should ask Slim to give you an interview. Talking to the press is part of what a musician does on a tour. It helps him get publicity."

Kit gulped. *Could I really be brave enough to do that?* Then she quickly put the thought out of her mind. She probably wouldn't even get the story— why worry about an interview?

"What else do you know about Slim that might make my pitch sound extra good?" Kit asked.

"Let's see," Dad said thoughtfully. "Ah, yes: two

things. First, Slim Simpson looks like a movie star, and he always dresses to the nines—he's known for it."

"He sounds dreamy! And what's the second thing?" Kit asked.

"Slim plays a King Liberty Silver Tone trumpet that he had custom-made," he said. "I've seen pictures of it. They designed a special sterling silver bell—that's the part of the trumpet where the sound comes out—covered with engravings of four-leaf clovers. There isn't another trumpet like it in the whole world. They say Slim's signature sound can only come from the bell of that Silver Tone."

"Wow," Kit said, her eyes wide. "It sounds just beautiful."

"So what do you think? Did you get enough for your pitch?" Dad asked.

"Oh yes," Kit said, her eyes shining as she stood up to hug her father. "I'm going to start working on it right now!"

...

The next afternoon after school, Kit gave her pitch as Mr. Gibson—or Gibb, as the reporters called him—listened patiently. She tried not to fidget or speak too quickly, reminding herself that it was important to remain professional and keep her excitement in check. When she finished, Gibb sat quietly. Though his office door was closed, the *clickety-clack* of many typewriters still filled the air. It was one of Kit's very favorite sounds, but she was too nervous to enjoy it. She couldn't tell a thing from Gibb's expression. Had her pitch gone well, or was he trying to figure out how to let her down easy?

"The thing is," Gibb began, "I know next to nothing about jazz. I heard about the concert, sure, but I hadn't thought about covering it. And you say yourself that those tickets sold out weeks ago."

As Gibb's voice trailed off, Kit sat up very

straight and still in her seat.

"And of course, it's not a children's story," Gibb added.

Kit nodded. *So he's going to say no. Don't look disappointed,* Kit told herself. *Just be grateful that he took the time to listen.* "I understand," she said. "Thank y—"

"On the other hand," Gibb continued, "the way you talk about Slim, it does sound like there could be a story here."

Kit froze again. Gibb began tapping his pencil on his desk.

This is worse than waiting to hear who won the tickets, Kit thought.

"Okay, here's what I think," Gibb said, dropping his pencil and leaning forward slightly. "I can't put one of my staff reporters on it even if I wanted to, since tickets are completely sold out. But you've got two front-row tickets, and you seem to know something about this guy. I'll tell you what, Kit."

It took every ounce of strength Kit had not to shout "*What?*"

"You're friendly with Miss Burns, the owner of the theater. She was nice about letting you hang around to research that Shakespeare production for us this summer. If she's willing to let you do that again, then by all means collect every detail you can from the moment Slim and his band hit town. Put something together for me. I can't make you any promises, but let's see what you come up with."

"Really?" Kit exclaimed. "I mean, that's terrific, Gibb! And if you really like it, you'll publish it in the children's section?"

Gibb gave Kit a funny look. "Well, no, Kit. I already told you we couldn't run a story like this in the children's section."

"Of course," Kit said quietly. She was confused. If Gibb wasn't going to publish it in the children's section, why would he encourage her to write the article at all?

"Like I said, put something together for me. Give it your very best. If it really grabs me, I'll publish it on our Metropolitan Page."

"Metropolitan Page?" Kit asked. "But that's . . . that's a staff reporter page. In the news section."

Gibb smiled. "Well, yes, it is."

Kit was speechless. Could Gibb really be giving her a shot at her first professional byline in the adult section of the paper? Every aspiring reporter dreamed of a chance like this!

"Remember, I can't guarantee I'll publish it," Gibb said. "But if I do, I'll pay you five dollars."

Five whole dollars? Kit caught her breath. Ever since her dad had lost his job in the Great Depression, Kit's family had been doing all they could to earn money. They had even taken in paying boarders to bring in more money each month. Five more dollars would be a real prize.

"Oh, thank you so much," Kit said, standing up so quickly she almost turned her chair over. "I'll put everything I have into this article. I promise!"

Gibb chuckled. "I'm sure you will. And thank you, Kit, for the jazz lesson. Can't wait to see what you come up with."

"Me too!" Kit exclaimed, her face flushed with excitement as she pushed through the door and almost skipped through the newsroom toward the exit.

A shot at the Metropolitan Page! Kit couldn't wait to see the look on Dad's face when she told him.

I've got my work cut out for me, Kit told herself as she emerged from the brick office building. *All I have to do is find the story Gibb will love, and write it.*

And Kit knew it would have to be nothing less than the best thing she had ever written in her life.

chapter 2

Following the Music

AS SOON AS school was out the next afternoon, Kit hurried across town to the Burns Theater.

Kit had spent a whole week of her summer vacation at the theater working on an article about a play. But things had become complicated when money began disappearing from the box office, threatening to put the theater out of business. By helping to find the thief and get the money back, Kit had helped save the theater, and Miss Burns had been immensely grateful.

Now that she trusts me, Kit thought, *maybe she'll introduce me to the band—or even Swingin' Slim himself.* But she knew that she mustn't count her chickens before they were hatched.

14

Kit rounded the corner and looked up at the theater's marquee.

THE GREAT SWINGIN' SLIM SIMPSON
& HIS ORCHESTRA
SEPTEMBER 14—ONE NIGHT ONLY
SOLD OUT!

Kit grinned. To think that she might get to meet Swingin' Slim Simpson and his band members! She bounded toward the theater's front door but stopped short when she caught sight of the glass display case that usually held announcements for upcoming shows. The glass had been broken, and shattered pieces littered the sidewalk. Someone had taken a poster out of the case, torn it to pieces, and left them scattered amid the broken glass.

Kit tiptoed around the pieces of sharp glass to inspect what remained of the poster. One piece said, "Swingin' Slim Simpson—in person!" in big bold letters. Another said, "Opening performance by Dizzy Dex Baxter."

Why would somebody do such a thing? Kit wondered. *I should tell Miss Burns right away.*

She tried the main door that led to the lobby, but it was locked. Kit knew from the time she'd spent at the theater that summer that the locked door likely meant that Miss Burns was off doing a quick errand or two. Kit didn't mind waiting on the sidewalk until she returned.

As she looked again at the damage to the display, Kit heard a distant honking sound. At first she thought it was a car down the street, but when she looked, she saw that the street was empty except for a few people walking and on bicycles. She heard the sound again and realized that it wasn't coming from the street, but from inside the theater.

Kit walked around the corner of the building and saw that the stage door was propped open with a chair. She knew the theater tended

to smell dusty and stale if it wasn't aired out
as often as possible, and since there were no windows backstage, Miss Burns frequently kept the
door open like this. Had Miss Burns forgotten
to close it when she left the theater? Someone was
definitely inside. Could the person who broke the
display case and tore up the poster have noticed
the open door and slipped through?

I'll sneak in and look, Kit decided. She felt con-
fident that she could stay out of sight. She knew
the theater so well, she could find her way around
backstage blindfolded.

When Kit stepped from the bright sunlight into
the dark theater, it did feel like she was wearing
a blindfold. She couldn't see a thing. As she waited
for her eyes to adjust, she heard the honk again.
This time it sounded familiar, running smoothly
up the scale from low notes to high. Kit almost
laughed out loud. It wasn't a car horn that she
had heard. It was a brass horn. A trumpet. And

that could mean only one thing.

Swingin' Slim Simpson was here!

Kit crept toward the stage to investigate, slipping in between the many layers of curtains in the wings where actors and dancers usually waited to take the stage. A single hanging work light illuminated the stage. Standing front and center was a brown-haired man with long, skinny legs and arms. He was holding a trumpet in one hand, fiddling with one of the valves.

He certainly doesn't look like a movie star from behind, Kit thought. *Of course, he isn't dressed up for a show and he doesn't know he has an audience.*

Then he put the trumpet to his lips, took a deep breath, and began to play.

Kit's mouth dropped open.

He was playing a tune so fast that Kit could barely distinguish one note from the next. He slid through the notes at lightning speed. One minute he careened down the scale. The next minute

he went up, the highest notes making a buzzing
sound that reminded Kit of a mosquito's whine. His
fingers moved over the three keys so fast they were
simply a blur, and he barely stopped for a breath.

How in the world does he do that? she thought.

He finished on a long high note, and Kit lifted
her hands to clap, remembering just in time that
she had to keep quiet. She didn't have permission
to be here, not yet!

The man lowered the trumpet, and silence fell
over the theater, broken only by a soft "oh," as if
someone had gasped. The trumpet player had
turned as if to walk offstage in the other direction,
but suddenly he spun back, looking directly into
the wings where Kit stood hidden between the
curtains. Kit's heart began to pound. Had he heard
the noise too?

"Hey. Hey you, kid! How did you get in here?"
he called, pointing in Kit's direction and scowling.
"Nobody's allowed in here! Come on, speak up!"

Kit's hands were shaking. Darn it—she had really meant to ask Miss Burns for official permission to be in the theater. *I'm going to have to tell the truth*, Kit told herself. *If I lose the story, I'll just have to learn from my mistake.*

She took a deep breath, then reached out to push the curtain away and reveal herself. But before her fingers even touched the curtain's soft, heavy velvet, she saw it move. Kit was astonished to see a girl around her age step out from the curtains just a few feet away. She wore a red dress, sunglasses, and a large hat and had long, dark hair pulled back with a white ribbon. Suddenly the girl bolted, flying down the steps leading from the stage and making a beeline for the fire door that opened directly outside.

"Where are you going, kid? I'm talking to you!" the man shouted. But the door slammed behind the girl and she was gone. The trumpeter shook his head, muttered something Kit couldn't hear, and walked right past her to go backstage.

Now seemed like an extremely good time to go see if Miss Burns had returned. Her heart still pounding, Kit quietly slipped from between the curtains and tiptoed down the steps, up the aisle, and through the double doors that led to the main lobby. Miss Burns had just come in from the street. As Kit quietly eased the lobby door closed, Miss Burns looked at her with surprise.

"Well, hello, Kit. How on earth did you get inside?" Miss Burns asked.

"I'm so sorry," Kit said quickly. "I was waiting for you on the sidewalk when I heard noises inside, and I saw someone had propped the stage door open. I was a little worried because somebody smashed the glass display outside. I thought I ought to investigate."

"Oh, can you believe someone's done that?" Miss Burns asked, shaking her head with dismay. "Can you imagine if the display were to look like that when Mr. Simpson arrives? My word, that would be a disaster."

Kit gave a little cry of dismay. "Oh, but he has arrived, Miss Burns!" she said. "The sound I went inside to investigate—it was Swingin' Slim. He was onstage, practicing!"

"Are you sure?" Miss Burns asked. "His manager told me he wouldn't be arriving until tomorrow. I expect it's just one of the other players, or perhaps the musician who will be opening for Slim. Well, if there is someone there, I should head into the theater to welcome him. I just hope he didn't notice the smashed display case."

Kit hated to see Miss Burns looking so upset. "I'm sure everyone will understand," Kit said. "It's not your fault if some vandals are causing mischief."

Miss Burns sighed. "I suppose that's true."

Just then Kit remembered why she had come to visit Miss Burns in the first place. "Miss Burns?

The reason I came to see you was—" she hesitated.

Miss Burns looked up at Kit and gave her a gentle smile. "Please, Kit. You can ask me anything," she pressed.

Feeling hopeful, Kit eagerly told Miss Burns about the tickets she'd won and the offer Gibb had made. "Would it be all right if I spent some time around the theater after school this week to research my article? I promise not to be a bother."

"Of course you may," Miss Burns said. "As long as none of Mr. Simpson's people mind, you may spend as much time here as you like, Kit."

"Oh, thank you!" Kit exclaimed. "And I'll keep my eyes open. If the vandals come back to the theater, I'm going to catch them in the act!"

chapter 3
A New Source

KIT SAID GOOD-BYE to Miss Burns and started toward home. She was thrilled that she had gotten permission to spend time at the theater and hoped that she would get to interview the band's crew or possibly a couple of the band members. Or even Slim!

Just then a flash of red near the little park across the street caught her eye. A girl in a red dress waited patiently in line as a pretzel peddler used tongs to pull a big pretzel off a hook for the customer in front of her. The girl's back was to Kit. Her long, dark hair was tied with a white ribbon.

Was it the girl from the theater?

Curious, Kit crossed the street as fast as she could without actually running. As she approached,

Kit saw the girl step up to the cart and ask for a pretzel as she handed over a nickel.

"One delicious pretzel coming right up! Extra salt!" the pretzel man said.

"Hello," Kit said to the girl in her friendliest voice, a big smile on her face.

The girl turned around to face Kit. She smiled back at Kit, but her eyes looked uncertain. Her sunglasses were pushed up on the top of her head, and she held a big hat under one arm.

"Hi. Um . . . do we know each other?"

Kit shook her head, still smiling.

"No, I just—I saw you in the theater."

The girl froze, the smile fading from her face. Kit thought she might actually turn and run, but the girl had already given the pretzel man her money.

"Don't worry," Kit added quickly. "I only saw you because I sneaked into the theater too!"

The girl tilted her head to one side, fixing Kit with a curious look. Then she arched one eyebrow.

Kit couldn't help but laugh.

"Let me start over. My name is Kit Kittredge. Miss Burns, who owns the theater, is a friend of mine. I went to the theater to scout out a story about Saturday's concert for the local paper."

"My name is Trixie. It's nice to meet you, Kit," said the girl as the man handed her a pretzel wrapped in paper. She gestured toward a bench at the park entrance, and the girls went to sit down. "So what do you mean, you went to scout out a story?"

"I'm a reporter," Kit said proudly. "I'm going to write a story about Swingin' Slim Simpson. I won tickets to his show on Saturday."

Trixie's eyes widened.

"I only went to the theater today to talk to Miss Burns, though. I had no idea he was already there!"

"Who was already where?" Trixie asked.

"Swingin' Slim. Practicing up on the stage at the theater," Kit explained, thinking what odd questions Trixie asked. "Miss Burns said she wasn't expecting him until tomorrow, but it must have been him."

"Oh, that wasn't Swingin' Slim Simpson," said Trixie matter-of-factly.

Kit tilted her head in confusion. "It wasn't?"

"No—that was Dizzy Dex Baxter." Trixie gave Kit a warm smile.

Kit felt her face turn hot. "Gosh, I'm so embarrassed. He just sounded so good! I didn't think too many people in the world would be able to play the trumpet like that!"

"Don't feel embarrassed. Dex is one of the best, too. But they have different styles. See, even if you'd never seen Slim, you'd know him by his sound. Slim has a custom-made trumpet, and he's known for his ability to change his sound—he can grab a high, clear sound one moment, and then he goes into whisper tones and you almost have to lean in to hear him. And nobody can make a trumpet growl like Swingin' Slim. Dizzy Dex is technically really good, but he'll never match Slim's sound."

"Golly!" Kit exclaimed, giving Trixie an admiring look. "How do you know so much about jazz? You sound almost like my dad!"

Trixie laughed as she popped a bite of pretzel into her mouth.

"I don't know. Listening to records, mostly. I've got lots of jazz records and a Victrola to play them on. And I read concert reviews and interviews. Swingin' Slim's tour just had a big write-up in *Jazz Time* magazine—and pages of pictures!"

"Really?" Kit asked. "I've got to find that magazine. I've never seen a picture of him."

Trixie grinned, her eyes sparkling. "Obviously. It sure is a good thing you didn't call Dizzy Dex 'Slim' by mistake."

"Why?" Kit asked.

Trixie leaned forward and dropped her voice to a whisper.

"They're enemies. They hate each other!"

"Really? What makes you say that?"

"I read it in *Jazz Time*," Trixie replied.

Trixie explained that Dex and Slim had moved to Chicago around the same time, hoping to make it big. "One day," she continued, "the famous Baron Van Buren Orchestra came to town, but on opening night the lead trumpet player got sick. So Van Buren scrambled to find the best trumpet player in Chicago to fill in, and he kept hearing the same two names: Dizzy Dex and Swingin' Slim. He picked Slim, and that ended up being Slim's big break. But Dex thought the spot should have gone to him." Trixie leaned in and lowered her voice as if she was about to share a secret with Kit. "Some people say they were both supposed to audition, and Slim tricked Dex into missing it. They've been rivals ever since."

Kit scribbled in her notebook as fast as she could. Trixie was a gold mine of information!

"But if they're rivals, what is Dizzy Dex doing here?" Kit asked.

"He's the opening act!" said Trixie. "I know, it seems strange that Slim would have his rival open for him. But he's a professional, and Dex has chops."

"He has chops?" Kit asked.

"Yeah. That means he can really play. Slim only wants the best musicians, even for his opening act," Trixie explained, her eyes sparkling. "That's going to be a killer show. I'd give anything to see it."

"You aren't going?" Kit asked.

Trixie shook her head. "I've been saving and saving, and I finally had enough for a ticket. But when I got to the theater, no one was in the box office and the marquee said that the concert was sold out. I was pretty disappointed, but then I heard Dex warming up. Actually, that's why I sneaked into the theater. You are so lucky you won tickets, Kit. You'll tell me all about it the next day, won't you?"

"Of course I will," Kit replied. "But I have a better idea, Trixie. You know so much about jazz and about Slim. And Miss Burns is letting me hang around the theater after school to research my story for the paper. Would you like to help?"

Trixie's mouth dropped open. "Are you kidding? Of course!" she exclaimed. Then her face fell. "But I wouldn't want to be in the way. Musicians are touchy about that sometimes. Maybe I could kind of stay in the background in the theater, and then help you with your article when we're alone."

"That sounds great," Kit said. "I'm going to be at the theater tomorrow after school. Do you think you could meet me there? Around three-thirty?"

"In the theater? Do you think Swingin' Slim will be there?"

"Well, Miss Burns told me that he's supposed to arrive tomorrow," Kit said. "But I don't want to bother him or anything on his first day. If I get a chance later, I'm going to ask if I can set up an interview, but I know he's there to do a job, so I don't want to get in his way."

"That sounds really smart," Trixie said. "We'll

stay out of Slim's way—he won't even know we're there. Oh Kit, I'm so glad I met you!" Trixie added, her face shining.

"Me too," Kit agreed.

Just then, they heard someone calling Trixie's name. The girls looked around and saw a woman down the street waving in their direction.

"Oh, that's my mom!" Trixie said, getting up. "I told her I'd meet her here after school to walk home together."

"Do you live close by?" Kit asked.

Trixie thought for a moment as if she wasn't sure how to answer. "We used to. Now we live in an apartment over on Braverman Avenue. But this park is on the way home from the store where my mom works."

"Trixie, let's go," her mother called.

"I'd better run," Trixie said with a grin. "See you tomorrow, Kit!"

"See you tomorrow!" Kit echoed.

...

At the dinner table that night, Kit's parents
and the boarders seemed quite captivated by her
retelling of the day's adventures. "I might even
get to meet Swingin' Slim Simpson tomorrow,"
Kit added.

"Kit, I do hope you keep in mind that your
homework and your chores must take priority over
your writing projects," Mother said as she cleared
Mrs. Howard's plate from the table.

Sitting next to Mrs. Howard was her son Stirling,
a boy in Kit's class, who had been squirming in his
seat and trying to catch Kit's eye ever since they'd
sat down for dinner.

Kit squinted at Stirling before turning back to
her mother. "I know," Kit assured her. "I won't let
my research get in the way, I promise."

"I'm counting on that," Mother said.

"Speaking of homework," said Mrs. Howard,

"perhaps you and Stirling had better get started. Kit, I'll help your mother with the dishes tonight."

"Thank you, Mrs. Howard," said Mother. "Kids, why don't you take your things onto the porch. The smell of fall is in the air. Soon it will be too chilly in the evening for you to work there."

"Yes, thank you, Mrs. Howard," Kit said, happy to be spared her usual chore of drying and putting away all the dinner dishes. "Come on, Stirling."

Kit and Stirling carried their books out to the screened porch. Kit curled up in a chair with her arithmetic book on her lap and began puzzling over a particularly challenging long-division problem, but she was distracted by Stirling, who seemed to be itching to tell her something.

She sighed. "Okay, Stirling, what is it?"

Stirling crossed the porch and plopped down in a chair across from Kit.

"When I went to return the extra papers left over from my delivery route today, I heard the

mailroom guys talking about something very interesting." Stirling had a job delivering newspapers for
the *Cincinnati Herald*, one of the other papers in town.

"What were they saying?" Kit asked, closing
her math book. Long division could wait another
few minutes.

"Someone sent in an anonymous letter to the
editor," Stirling said.

"What's so interesting about that?" Kit asked.
"The *Register* gets letters to the editor all the time,
and a lot of people don't sign their names."

"But this letter was about Swingin' Slim
Simpson," Stirling replied.

Kit perked up. "Did you actually see this letter?"

Stirling shook his head. "No, but my friend
Bobby did. He said it was handwritten and really
long. It was some kind of protest about the Burns
Theater booking Swingin' Slim Simpson for that
concert. It said Slim was a person . . . how exactly
did he say it? A person of 'bad character and ill

repute.' That's it," Stirling said, looking pleased with himself for remembering. "It criticized Miss Burns for bringing someone 'like that' to our neighborhood. And it said something about a problem Slim had with other musicians, cheating or getting into fights or something, and then it started to talk about some other bad thing Slim had done, but that's as far as Bobby read."

"I can't believe someone would write something like that, attacking Slim and Miss Burns," Kit said. "Something like that could really hurt her if it was printed—people have no way of knowing the truth. It's a good thing that letter will never be printed."

"It won't?" Stirling asked. "How do you know?"

"It's newspaper policy that a letter can only be printed if the author gives the newspaper his or her name and address, even if that person wants the letter signed as 'anonymous' when it is published," she told Stirling. "Otherwise, people could say anything at all and not be responsible for it."

"Well, then, it's a relief that the letter about Slim won't get printed, I guess," said Stirling.

Kit nodded. "But still, who would write such a letter?" It seemed as if Mr. Slim Simpson might have enemies. If so, Kit intended to find out who they were.

chapter 4

Cast of Characters

KIT SKIPPED UP the block toward the theater.
Today was the day she could begin researching her
article in earnest.

And there was Trixie, wearing her big hat again,
waiting by the theater's main entrance and looking
down the street.

"Trixie, hi!" Kit called, walking quickly toward
her friend.

Trixie looked up and around, catching sight of
Kit. She pulled her hat off. For a moment, Trixie had
an odd expression on her face, as if she was nervous
or frightened. Then it was gone.

"Are you okay?" Kit asked.

Trixie nodded quickly. "Just eager to get inside."

Kit looked over to the display where she had

seen the torn-up poster. Someone had swept away the glass and covered the empty frame with brown paper. It looked shabby, but Kit had to admit that this was better than leaving the damage for all to see.

"It's too bad about the display case," Kit said. "It must have been a couple of pranksters causing trouble."

Trixie just bit her lip and didn't say anything.

Boy, she must be really nervous to meet Slim, Kit thought. She nudged Trixie. "Come on," she urged. "Let's go find Miss Burns."

The door to Miss Burns's office was cracked open, and Kit cautiously peeked inside. Miss Burns was sitting on the swivel chair behind her desk, the telephone pressed to her ear. A man with a mop of chocolate-colored hair sat opposite her, his back to the door.

I recognize that hair, Kit realized. *That's Dizzy Dex Baxter!*

"Yes, I understand," Miss Burns was saying into the phone. "But several of the music stands were loaded onto the wrong truck. I've tracked them down, and I've been told they're on their way here, but I wanted to let you know about the mix-up."

As Kit and Trixie stepped into the doorway, the man turned and looked at them. Trixie gave a little gasp. Dex looked straight at Trixie and chuckled. "Well, if it isn't the little intruder I found hiding in the stage curtains yesterday!"

Miss Burns drew the phone's mouthpiece away from her face and looked at Kit and Trixie. "Intruder?"

Trixie looked at the floor and stuttered, "I . . . well, you see—"

"She was with me," Kit said, covering for Trixie. "I came to talk to Miss Burns, and we saw you onstage. Trixie here was so anxious about seeing a famous musician in person that she couldn't even remember her own name when you spoke to her. Isn't that right, Trix?"

Trixie looked at Kit gratefully. "Uh, yes. That's right. I was . . . really nervous."

Dex threw his head back and laughed. "Famous musician, huh? Thanks, kid. You just made my day! Usually it's only our pretty boy Slim who gets recognized."

"He's not here, is he?" Trixie asked.

"Nope, just boring old me, I'm afraid," he said. "And who are you?"

Trixie looked around for Kit and pulled her forward.

"I'm nobody important, but this is Kit Kittredge, and she's writing a story about the concert for the newspaper."

"Ah, the press!" Dex exclaimed. "Good to know. I'll be on my best behavior."

Miss Burns turned her attention back to her call. "Yes, all right, that will be fine," she responded before hanging up. "Well, Kit, I see you've already met Mr. Baxter."

"Please, call me Dex."

"It's nice to meet you," Kit said. "And Miss Burns, this is my friend Trixie. She knows lots about jazz. Would it be okay if she helped me research my story?"

"As long as Mr. Baxter—-Dex, I mean—and Mr. Simpson don't object, you're both welcome," Miss Burns replied. "Now, if you'll excuse me, I have a long to-do list that I must get started on."

Dex stood up. "Yeah, sorry I had to pester you about that, but we need those stands. Thanks for letting me know they're on the way. Some of the band members are already here, checking out the acoustics. Are either of you reporters interested in meeting a few of them?"

Kit could hardly contain her excitement, but she told herself, *You are here on business. You must be professional if you want to be a real reporter.* She suppressed the urge to jump up and down and instead stood up a little straighter.

"That would be very kind of you, thank you," said Kit calmly.

"I don't want to be in the way," Trixie said, looking down. "I've read that Mr. Simpson doesn't like to be bothered when he's setting up."

"Well, that's true. But like I said, Slim's not here yet," Dex said. "If you're game, follow me."

"Come on, Trix. Don't you want to meet the other musicians?" Kit asked.

Trixie's face broke into a smile, and she nodded. "Do I ever!" she whispered.

Kit and Trixie followed Dex through the lobby to the double doors that opened into the auditorium. The stage was abuzz with activity. A group of men were constructing some kind of platform on the stage.

"What are they all doing?" Kit asked, pulling her notebook from her pocket and checking her pencil to make sure it was sharp.

"Well, the guys in the back are building a platform for Boogie-Woogie Jones," Dex replied.

"Wow, Boogie-Woogie Jones?" Trixie asked. She turned to Kit, who gave a little giggle at the silly name. "He's Slim's drummer."

"You really know your stuff," Dex said, nodding. "People like to see Boogie-Woogie perform, so he gets his own little platform. In front of that, they'll put a riser for the back tier of musicians. See, Slim likes to put his trumpet players in the back row, because he thinks if they're in the front it's hard to hear the rest of the instruments. But if you do that, the saxophone and trombone players in front complain about having all those trumpets pointed right at the backs of their heads! So he puts us on risers, so that we're up a little higher. But if you ask me, Slim is flat-out wrong, and the trumpet players should sit front and center."

Kit sensed a bit of resentment in his voice, and she remembered what Trixie had said about Dex

and Slim's tense relationship. Was she getting
a glimpse of the rivalry now?

"Typical trumpet player, always wanting the
glory," came a low, gravelly voice.

Kit turned around and saw a big, bald-headed
man holding the largest and shiniest horn she'd
ever seen.

"Typical honker, always gotta be the heavy,"
Dex retorted with a good-natured grin. "Kit and
Trixie, I'd like you to meet Hootie Shay. Watch what
you say, Hoot. They may look like just a couple of
kids, but these two are putting together a story for
the newspaper."

"Don't worry about me," Hootie said. "You're
the one always shooting his mouth off to reporters
about how Slim Simpson stole your big shot at star-
dom." He winked at the girls. "Don't let him pick
any fights with you, kids—Dex can be a real prickly
pear sometimes. Nice to meet you, girls."

"Nice to meet you too," Kit said. "I'm sorry to

ask a dumb question, but what kind of instrument is that?"

"This is a baritone saxophone," Hootie told Kit, holding it up and looking as proud as if it were a baby.

Like saxophones Kit had seen in magazines, it was a shiny, tube-shaped instrument bent back on itself in a tight U-shape, flaring out at the end in a wide bell. When Hootie held it with the mouthpiece near his chin, the bottom of the instrument stretched almost to his knees.

"It's so big!" Kit exclaimed. "I thought saxophones were smaller."

"Most of them are," Hootie told her. "But a bari sax has a real deep tone, and the deeper the tone, the bigger the instrument. Tenors and altos are smaller. And a soprano sax is just a little thing—it looks more like a clarinet. I can play all of them, but I like the big bari sax sound the best."

He lifted the instrument to his lips and played

a soulful tune that Kit recognized from the King
Jazz Hour radio show. The sound of the instrument
was so deep and powerful that Kit felt it vibrating
in her chest. When he stopped playing, Kit's ears
were ringing.

"It sounds like a foghorn!" she exclaimed.

"Everybody's a critic," Hootie said, laughing.
"Hey, Dex, it looks like we're a few music stands
short. Anyone tracking them down? I'd really hate
to spend the afternoon putting a fresh coat of paint
on the spares."

"The theater manager, Miss Burns, already took
care of it," Dex replied. "They're on their way here."

"Terrific," Hootie said. "I'm gonna run across
the street and grab a pretzel. See you later, girls!"

"What's he doing?" Trixie asked, pointing to
a man with a paintbrush who sat on the floor in
front of a row of music stands. "I thought you didn't
need to paint the spares."

"Just a little touch-up painting," Dex said,

gesturing for the girls to follow him as he walked down the aisle toward the stage. As they came closer, Kit could see that each stand had a long wooden front adorned with Swingin' Slim's logo: three swirly *S* patterns that curled into one another like snakes. "Slim likes them all to look perfect, and for once we've got some extra time. Usually we arrive at a gig the day before or the day of. But Slim wanted to make sure the stage checked out, which is why I arrived a day ahead of the rest of the band."

"What were you checking the stage for?" Kit asked.

"Well, when you play a music club, certain things go without saying," Dex explained. "You know the place is set up for a band. The mikes are gonna work, acoustics will be good—no surprises. But when you play a theater like this one, you never know. I played a gig once at an old vaudeville house. The place looked like it might fall down around our ears. So in the middle of the show, this trumpet player named Stan jumped off the riser because he was supposed to come down front and do a vocal. And Stan was a really big guy, you know what I mean? Never missed a meal. So Stan jumped off the riser and he went right through the stage floor, all the way up to his waist! And he was stuck there, still holding his trumpet. I have never laughed so hard in my life. We had to stop the concert. It took fifteen minutes to get him out of that hole!"

Kit and Trixie exchanged amazed looks as they laughed.

"You won't have anything like that to worry about here," Kit said. "This is an old theater too, but Miss Burns takes great care to keep it in good shape!"

"I hope so," Dex said, stopping at the front row a few feet from the stage. "There's gonna be a lot of musicians up there."

"How many musicians are in the band?" Kit asked.

"About twenty," Dex said. "You've got trumpets, trombones, saxophones, a couple of clarinets, Boogie-Woogie Jones and his drum kit, plus an upright bass and a piano. Can get awfully tight in a small space. I once played a room so small, when the slide trombone hit a high note it knocked the horn right out of my hand."

Kit was writing furiously in her notebook when she heard a woman's booming voice say, "Dexter Baxter, are you plying these young ladies with your tall tales again?"

Kit looked up and saw a towering golden-haired woman in a blue skirt and huge broad-shouldered jacket walking confidently across the stage.

"Nah, these are my regular-sized tales," Dex said. "I've gotta work my way up to the tall ones. Kit and Trixie, meet the one and only Lady Deedles—queen of the ivory ticklers and canary extraordinaire. Do not mess with her."

"Oh," Kit said, feeling utterly foolish because she didn't know what an ivory tickler or a canary was. "It's nice to meet you."

Trixie noticed that Kit's pencil had paused next to Lady Deedles's name in her notebook. She leaned over and whispered, "He means that she plays the piano and sings in Slim's band."

"Wow," Kit said. "A woman piano player?" She immediately blushed, realizing she was being rude. "I mean, oh, that came out wrong. I just don't really hear a lot of women's names when I listen to the radio," she murmured.

"Oh, I don't mind!" Lady Deedles exclaimed. "I worked hard to get where I am. And it's true, you don't see many female musicians in the big bands. I expect one day all that will change." She winked at the girls before looking around the theater. "Well, I think this is going to be a nice gig. I like this place."

"I suppose it's okay," Dex said. "But I still don't

understand what we're doing at a no-name joint in Cincinnati in the first place."

Kit looked up in surprise, and Lady Deedles nudged Dex and frowned.

"Not that there's anything wrong with Cincy!" Dex added quickly. "It's a great city and all that, and I know it's Slim's hometown. I just figured we'd play a bigger place—the Music Hall or something. Lugging everything here for just the one night, to a gig with just a few hundred seats, I just don't get it. Even his own manager was trying to talk him out of it, but he wouldn't take no for an answer. Had to be this particular theater."

"Any idea why it had to be the Burns Theater?" Kit asked.

"Well, he ought to be here any minute. You can ask him yourself," Lady Deedles said.

"Oh!" Trixie exclaimed. Kit, Dex, and Lady Deedles all looked at her expectantly. "I'm sorry. It's just . . . I lost track of the time! I've got to help my mother with some things. She'll be cross with me if I keep her waiting. See you back here tomorrow, Kit?"

"Sure," Kit said, slightly taken aback by Trixie's sudden announcement. She hadn't said anything earlier about having to help her mother. "So then, we'll meet outside the theater again at three-thirty, okay?"

"Okay," Trixie called over her shoulder, bolting for the exit. Kit watched, puzzled, as Trixie pushed the fire door open and disappeared into the daylight.

Suddenly, Dex's attention turned to the lobby doors. "Oh boy," he muttered. "He's early. I'd better get hopping. See ya later, kid." He hopped up onto the stage and disappeared into the wings.

"Who's early?" Kit asked.

Lady Deedles pointed toward the back of the house. An elegant-looking man was walking down the aisle toward the stage, escorted by Miss Burns. He wore a stylish hat at a jaunty tilt, and a beautiful dark suit with sharp creases in the trousers. Just the sight of him took Kit's breath away.

There was no doubt about it. Swingin' Slim Simpson had arrived.

chapter 5

Slim

SLIM'S ARRIVAL HAD an instant effect on
everyone in the theater. The men putting the risers
together stopped hammering. The musicians who
were tuning their instruments stopped playing.
Although he hadn't said a word, Slim had the full
attention of everyone in the room.

Kit slipped quietly into one of the theater seats,
remembering what Trixie had said about Slim's
dislike of strangers getting in the way of setup and
rehearsal. She made herself as small as possible, all
the while never taking her eyes off Slim. He was
impossible *not* to watch. It wasn't just that he looked
like a movie star, with his elegant suit, raven-black
hair, and blazing blue eyes. It wasn't just that he
was famous. There was something else: Slim had

a way about him. He seemed to pulse with energy. *This must be what it means when they say someone has charisma*, Kit thought.

"Gentlemen!" Slim said cheerfully to the people gathered onstage. "And lady," he added, tipping his hat at Lady Deedles. "Glad to see we're all here. Or most of us. Where'd Dex run off to now? And how's the sound in this space? Hootie, play me a riff."

Hootie picked up his large saxophone and launched into an energetic version of something that sounded like "Twinkle, Twinkle, Little Star." Slim stood in the aisle, his hands on his hips, his head cocked to one side. Then he put his hand up, and Hootie stopped.

"Okay, hold on," Slim said, turning and walking to the back of the theater, to the very last row of seats. "Now play it again."

Hootie played the same tune, except at the end, there was a squawk where the last few notes should have been. Kit stifled a giggle.

"Oops," Hootie said. "Sorry—I've got a warped reed."

"The sound is traveling okay," Slim said, walking back down the aisle toward the stage. "But it's a little dead. Between the carpeting and all those heavy curtains, we're gonna lose some volume— even more when these seats are filled with people."

Kit was fascinated. There was so much more to being a bandleader than the average person would think.

Slim climbed the steps that led up onto the stage. He set down a little suitcase and opened it. The inside of the suitcase seemed to glow under the work light. Slim snapped a velvet strap and pulled out his trumpet.

The King Liberty Silver Tone.

I can't believe I'm this excited over a trumpet, Kit thought, almost laughing out loud. But as Slim stood onstage, the trumpet in his hand bathed in light, Kit felt as if she was seeing something truly special.

Slim connected the mouthpiece to the horn's body. He put the trumpet to his lips and played a scale, lingering on the last note. Trixie was right. The sound that came out of Slim's trumpet sounded smoother and clearer to her than any note Dex—or any other horn player she'd heard on the radio—had ever played.

Slim scratched his chin and said, "Miss Burns, do you have some stage flats that can be set up behind us? Anything smooth and hard the sound can bounce off will help."

"We do have stage flats," Miss Burns told him. "I can have my assistant set them up for you if a few of your people can help him." She nodded to her assistant, Graham, who stood at the back of the theater. Graham rushed down the aisle and hopped onto the stage before introducing himself to Slim.

"I'm happy to assist you, sir," he said, shaking Slim's hand. "And I have a new assistant who should be here any moment. He can help us with those stage flats."

"Terrific," Slim said, flashing a gleaming smile. "What about these curtains?" he asked, pointing to the heavy velvet curtains overhead. "Any chance they can come down?"

"I'm afraid not," Miss Burns said. "We can pull them back all the way, but to remove them would be a complicated process—we'd need scaffolding and a special crew."

Kit was able to pull her eyes away from Slim long enough to see that Dizzy Dex had returned. He soundlessly slipped into a seat in the front row and folded his arms over his chest, watching Slim.

"All right," Slim said. "But in that case, we'll have to lose the risers. The trumpets will still cut through just fine, but we're going to lose too much of the reeds if the horns play over their heads."

Graham nodded. "Right away, sir. I'll just run backstage to see if my assistant has arrived yet."

As Graham disappeared behind the curtain, Dex stood up and called to Slim. "Why make him do all this work when you can just put the trumpets in front?" he asked.

"Oh, there you are, Dex," Slim said. "Nice of you to join us. If I put the trumpets in front, as you know perfectly well, we'll lose even more of the reeds. There's not enough surface to bounce the sound off of in this house. Trumpets go in the back row, floor level."

"It's all the same to you," Dex said. "You'll be up on the bandstand."

"That's right," Slim said. "Because I'm the boss."

Kit sank even lower in her seat, embarrassed to be witnessing this sparring between Slim and Dex. Dex just shrugged and smiled, as if the whole thing were a joke.

Just then Graham returned with a short man in a plaid cap carrying a large piece of plywood with a wooden frame. They huffed and puffed as they maneuvered their way across the stage with the unwieldy frame. The man helping Graham hoisted the frame upward to try to get a better grip, sending his plaid cap off his bald head and onto the floor.

Slim quickly placed his trumpet back in its case, slipped off his jacket, and handed both to Hootie. "Would you stash my things in the greenroom for me, please?" he asked. "It looks like they'll need some help getting these stage flats set up."

"Sure thing, boss," Hootie said, taking the jacket and trumpet case and heading offstage.

Slim rushed to assist with the stage flats, and the men were able to hoist the frame upright behind the drummer's platform. Slim brushed his hands on his pants with satisfaction, looking around the stage before squinting toward the back of the house. He seemed to be measuring every detail of the theater. Kit realized with a start that his gaze had suddenly fixed directly on her.

"And who do we have here?" Slim asked,

walking to the edge of the stage to get a better look at Kit. "An unannounced audition? Let me guess. Singer? Pianist? Don't tell me you're a tap dancer—I can't have some adorable little Shirley Temple stealing the stage from my band!"

Kit felt heat rush to her face and was momentarily tongue-tied as everyone in the theater stared at her. Miss Burns walked quickly up the aisle and placed a hand on Kit's shoulder.

"This is Kit Kittredge, the young reporter I was telling you about, Mr. Simpson," Miss Burns said.

Slim skipped lightly down the stairs from the stage to the floor and approached Kit, his hand extended. Somehow she managed to stand up. "Nice to meet you, Kit Kittredge," he said, flashing his dazzling smile. "I understand you'd like to hang around and see what we do."

"If it's all right with you," Kit said, her voice coming out higher and faster than she meant it to. "I promise I won't get in anyone's way."

"I'm sure you won't," Slim said, his bright blue eyes sparkling. "There won't be much to see today. We're just getting set up. But tomorrow we'll be rehearsing our numbers. You're welcome to listen in."

Kit's heart was still beating fast, but Slim's manner was so friendly, her nervousness began to slip away.

"Oh yes," Kit said. "I would love to!"

"Sure thing, kid," Slim said. "I always have time for my friends in the press."

She was about to ask Slim if he would have time for an interview as well when Hootie Shay called to him from the stage. "Hey, Slim, the house piano's got a few sticky keys, and Lady Deedles won't let anyone touch it until you go backstage and try it yourself."

Slim laughed. "Poor Deedles, she's the only one who can't bring along her own instrument," he told Kit. "She once played a gig with a piano that got all wonky if you played anything below the bass C. Turns out a cat had squeezed inside to have her kittens. Five of us went home with kittens after that gig."

"Hey, Slim," someone else called. "We need you over here!"

Slim nodded and turned back to Kit. "We'll see you tomorrow, then."

Kit hesitated. Slim was obviously very busy. *But this might be my only chance to ask him,* she told herself. *The worst he can do is say no.*

"One more thing," she said, standing a little taller. "I was hoping if you had the time, you might be able to give me a short interview?"

"Rehearsal starts tomorrow at four," Slim told her. "Can you be at the coffee shop next door at three-thirty?"

"Yes! That would be great!" Kit said.

Slim gave her another brilliant smile.

"I'll see you then, Kit Kittredge," he said. As he turned to climb the steps onto the stage, he shouted:

"Hootie! Pitch in a hand to help the fellas put up those flats, okay? And where's Deedles? Has she checked the piano's soundboard?" Everyone converged on Slim, all of them talking at once.

Miss Burns squeezed Kit's arm. "You got your interview!"

Kit put her hand over her mouth. "I almost didn't ask," she said. "I was so nervous. He's so busy and important!"

"And so handsome," Miss Burns said as she walked with Kit up the aisle toward the lobby. "My goodness, he's every bit as dashing as Clark Gable!"

"Oh, I wish Trixie were still here," Kit said. "I've only got half an hour for the interview, so I need to come up with some really sharp questions. Trixie has read almost every interview Slim's ever given—she'd know some good questions to ask."

"It sounds like you have work to do," Miss Burns said, holding the door to the lobby open so Kit could go through. "And so do I. I had no idea what I was getting into when Slim's manager called to book this show. He promised me the concert would sell out easily, which it has, but there were so many things to work out. I had already booked a one-man play for the same weekend, but the deposit was never paid, so I had to cancel that. The actor was very cross about it. And I've only had plays performed here so far. I've never had an orchestra, so I had no idea how to prepare for them. Frankly, I was worried some of our older patrons might object to a jazz show. They might think I'm turning the theater into some kind of nightclub. It's a good thing we haven't had any damage since the broken display and torn-up poster yesterday. I don't think we could handle another incident."

Kit felt a guilty twinge in her stomach, thinking of the anonymous letter to the editor that Stirling had told her about. *Should I tell her about that?* Kit wondered. But she saw no point in worrying Miss

Burns about it. Kit waved good-bye and headed
out the theater's front door, almost tripping over a
wooden folding ladder lying on the sidewalk under
the marquee. She took one last look up at the marquee and stopped short.

"What in the world?" Kit asked out loud.

It looked as if someone had taken a big chalk-
board eraser and swept most of the letters in a
jumbled pile to the side. With the remaining letters,
the marquee now said:

GET OUT SLIM—OR ELSE!

chapter 6

Sabotage

KIT RAN INSIDE to get Miss Burns.

"What is it, Kit?" Miss Burns asked as she shuffled through some papers on her desk. "As you can see, I'm quite busy."

"There's something you need to see outside," Kit said, trying to remain composed. "It's really important."

Miss Burns saw the concerned look on Kit's face and calmly followed her to the sidewalk in front of the theater.

"My goodness!" Miss Burns exclaimed, staring up at the marquee.

"I'm sorry to worry you with this when you've already got so much to do," Kit said apologetically. "But I knew you'd want to take care of it right away."

"I most certainly do," Miss Burns replied. "Wait here a moment, will you? I'm going to run inside and get Graham right now. I just hope he isn't in the middle of something that Slim won't want interrupted."

Kit looked anxiously up and down the street. There were several trucks passing by, and a boy on a bike who did a double take at the marquee, looking away only when his front wheel began to wobble.

Oh, I do wish Graham would hurry!

As if on cue, the lobby door flew open and Graham rushed out, Miss Burns right behind him. He took one look at the marquee and whistled. Without a word, he dragged the wooden folding ladder from where it lay on the sidewalk and in one powerful movement, he swung it upright and snapped it open. "I'll take all the letters down," Graham called over his shoulder from the top of the ladder.

"Good," Miss Burns said with a sigh of relief as the message disappeared letter by letter. "It's strange—I didn't see anything wrong when I arrived."

"It must have just happened," Kit said. "Because Slim didn't see anything amiss, or surely he would have said something. The ladder isn't always out here, is it?"

"Nope," Graham called. "Had it out so I could give the border a polish and replace one of the light-bulbs. But I got sidetracked when Mr. Simpson showed up. Sorry."

"It's not your fault, Graham," Miss Burns said firmly, pressing her lips together, a worried crease on her forehead. "But certainly this is troubling. Who would do this, and why?"

"I've got to get home—I've got chores to do and I'm already late," Kit said. "But I'm going to try to figure this all out, Miss Burns. Try not to worry."

Miss Burns gave Kit an encouraging smile. "Thank you, Kit. I suppose that's all I can do for now."

It was nice of her to say that, Kit thought as she

headed in the direction of her house. But the whole thing was giving Kit a very bad feeling.

Because she'd been late getting home, Kit barely had time to think about the strange message on the marquee. By the time she completed her chores and homework, it was dark outside. Nonetheless, she went out the front door and sat on the steps, her chin propped in her hand. Sometimes a little fresh air helped her think, and the brisk temperature encouraged her brain to move less toward sleep and more toward running the facts through her mind.

"Three things," Kit said, because saying things out loud also helped. "The ripped-up concert poster, the anonymous letter to the editor, and the message on the marquee."

"Do you and your invisible friend want to be alone?" came a voice from behind her.

Kit turned and made a face at Stirling, who

was standing in the doorway. "Very funny," she said. "I'm trying to make sense of something that, well, just doesn't make sense."

"Can I help?" Stirling asked eagerly, coming all the way outside before Kit could answer. "Is this about the concert? Don't tell me something else happened."

Kit sighed and nodded. She gave Stirling a brief rundown of the day's events.

Stirling shook his head in disbelief. "Well, it sounds like someone's out to make trouble for Swingin' Slim."

Stirling was right, Kit thought. But why this concert? Why now?

"All of this has happened in just a few days, and Slim's concert is on Saturday night," Kit said, thinking out loud. "There have been other performances at the theater this month, and other acts will come in after Saturday. So far, the things that have happened have been related only to Slim's concert."

Stirling narrowed his eyes and chewed on his lower lip.

"Okay," he said after a moment. "So unless we find something that proves otherwise, we'll assume that the same person is behind the anonymous letter, the torn poster, and the message on the marquee. Someone who . . . really hates jazz? And doesn't want the concert to go on?"

"But why?" asked Kit. "I mean, a person could go through life just hating opera but never once think about trying to sabotage a performance. Damaging theater property is a crime. Why break the law and risk getting caught just to make a point about music?"

Stirling frowned thoughtfully. "Well, when people commit crimes, it's usually for profit or revenge, right?"

"Right," Kit agreed. "And this doesn't seem to be about profit. I mean, who stands to profit by driving Slim out of town?"

"Right. So maybe it's revenge. And revenge is personal. What do you know about Slim's personal life?" Stirling asked.

"Just what I've put together for my article," Kit said. "He grew up here and became successful in Chicago. He's very handsome, and he's both talented and ambitious."

"Maybe there's someone from his past," Stirling suggested. "Someone from here—his hometown— who's been waiting all this time for a chance to even some score."

"Sure, but there's no way in the world for us to know who might have been mad at Slim Simpson for the last I don't know how many years," Kit replied.

Stirling looked undeterred. "Okay, then what about the people who work for him now? Do you think he's easy to work for, or is he a mean boss?"

Kit thought back to Slim's entrance today. "From the little that I saw today, it seemed like people have a lot of respect for him, and when he says jump they ask, 'How high?' From the moment he arrived at the theater, he was the focus of everyone's attention, and he was definitely running the show. I didn't see him do or say anything unkind, though."

"Hmm," Stirling said. "So far, he doesn't sound like the kind of guy who would have a bunch of enemies."

Something tugged at the edges of Kit's memory, then suddenly became clear. "Actually, there is one thing," she said. "The girl I met yesterday, Trixie, read an article in a magazine about a rivalry he has with another musician."

Stirling raised both eyebrows, and whistled. "A rivalry, huh? So at least that part of the letter was true."

"There's more," Kit added. "The man who's supposed to be Slim's rival is a trumpet player named Dizzy Dex, and he's here right now, in Cincinnati. Guess where?"

"At the Burns Theater?" Stirling asked.

"Exactly," Kit said. "Now that I think about it, he did disappear for a few minutes when Slim made his big entrance. And that would have been just around the time the sign on the marquee was tampered with."

"Well!" Stirling exclaimed. "It looks like Dizzy Dex just became your number one suspect! That's a start."

Kit nodded. But she couldn't help thinking that it wasn't a very good start, and time was running out—the concert was in two more days.

Later, when Kit had washed up, brushed her teeth, and put on her nightgown, she sat on her bed with her reporter's notebook in her lap. The notebook was opened to a page with the heading *Questions for Slim Simpson Interview*. After staring at it for a moment, she turned to the next page and wrote a new heading: *Suspects.*

And beneath that, she added,

1. Someone from Slim's past holding a grudge.

2. Dizzy Dex Baxter.

Kit chewed the end of her pencil thoughtfully. What if there really *was* someone from Slim's past out there who had been waiting to exact a terrible revenge? She knew that the interview was a huge opportunity to find out more about Slim. But between the goings-on at the theater and school tomorrow, she had very little time to prepare for it.

I must come up with a thorough list of questions, Kit told herself. *Even if it takes half the night.*

chapter 7

The Interview

KIT GLANCED UP at the clock above the blackboard and almost groaned out loud with dismay. How could the minutes be passing so slowly? Math never went quickly, especially since it was the last class of the day. But Kit was positive she'd actually seen the minute hand move *back* in time once or twice.

She slid her reporter's notebook slightly out from where it was hidden beneath her math book.

"All right, class," began the teacher, Mr. Scott. "Mr. Smith has walked 126 miles in the last two weeks. If he walked the same distance each day, how many miles a day has Mr. Smith walked?"

Kit tried to look like she was doing division in her head. But she couldn't focus.

Why can't someone just ask Mr. Smith how far he walked? Why doesn't Mr. Smith just take the bus?

Kit peeked at the open page in her reporter's notebook, where she had written the questions for Slim Simpson's interview.

1. When did you know you wanted to be a musician?

2. What is it like doing a national tour? Is it fun, or do you get tired of it?

3. What is the hardest thing about having your own band? What is the best thing?

4. I know the kind of jazz you play is called swing. In just a few words, how would you describe it?

5. What made you decide to come to the Burns Theater?

6. Who do you—

Kit's train of thought was interrupted by her teacher's voice. "Come on, children, I'm not seeing many hands up. Kit?"

Kit's head jerked up. "Yes, Mr. Scott?"

"Mr. Smith went 126 miles in two weeks. How many miles is that a day?"

The question just seemed so silly at the moment, when all she could think about was jazz. Kit looked down and caught sight of her second interview question. Instead of Mr. Smith, she imagined it was Slim's band, traveling from town to town to play their gigs. She frowned as she thought, and then looked up hopefully. "Nine?"

Mr. Scott rewarded her with a smile. "Very good," he said. "I should call more often on people who don't raise their hands."

"Thanks a *lot*," whispered Stirling, who was sitting behind her. Stirling rarely raised his hand.

Kit made a shushing gesture behind her back. Mr. Scott was very strict, and he didn't like note passing, talking in class, or students who weren't prepared to answer questions. The school year had only just begun, and Kit did *not* want to get on his bad side. In fact, Mr. Scott often gave students who didn't pay attention after-school detention!

I'll have barely enough time to walk to the coffee shop when the last bell rings—if I get detention, I'll miss the interview!

Kit slid her reporter's notebook out of sight and fixed Mr. Scott with what she hoped was an interested and attentive look. It wasn't easy, but she managed to keep it up for the rest of class, and he did not call on her again.

When the bell rang, Kit practically shouted for joy. Stirling leaned over his desk as she hastily shoved her schoolbooks into her bag. "Good luck with the interview," he said.

"Thanks, Stirling." Kit flashed him a smile and squeezed her notebook to her chest. "I'll tell you all about it when I get home."

...

Kit had to walk her fastest to get to the coffee shop by three-thirty. Gibb had told her that one of the most unprofessional things a reporter could do was to be late for an interview. Kit was determined never to let that happen to her.

Oh no, Kit thought, slapping her hand to her forehead. She had told Trixie to meet her outside the theater at three-thirty. Being on time for Slim meant she wouldn't have a chance to tell Trixie why she couldn't meet her. Well, there was nothing to be done about it. When Trixie found out why Kit was delayed, surely she'd understand.

A little bell rang on the coffee shop door as Kit pushed it open. A white-haired man behind a glass case of pastries smiled and waved. "Take a table anywhere you like, miss," he called.

"Thank you," Kit said, choosing one by the window. She looked out at the street outside, wiggling her foot nervously. Would Slim remember the appointment?

When the waitress came, Kit ordered a hot chocolate. The waitress scribbled something on her pad and then stared at Kit expectantly.

"Something to go with that? Sandwich? Soup? Slice of pie?"

"No, thank you," Kit said. "Just the hot chocolate."

The waitress sighed loudly and walked away, muttering something under her breath about kids.

Don't let her get to you, Kit said to herself. But as she picked up her notebook to look over her questions for the hundredth time, she noticed that her hands were shaking. *You don't want to look like a scared little kid,* she told herself sternly. She practiced taking slow, deep breaths, but when she heard the bell on the door jangle, she jumped a little. It was Slim. He *had* remembered!

"Right on time, Miss Kit Kittredge, just as I expected you'd be," Slim said, sitting down at the table opposite her. He was clean-shaven, and his black hair was perfectly combed. He was wearing another beautiful suit, and the sort of hat Kit saw businessmen wearing on their way to work.

"Thank you so much for coming," Kit said, folding her hands in her lap so he wouldn't see that they were shaking.

The waitress returned to the table and set a steaming mug of hot chocolate in front of Kit.

"And what can I get for you, sir? Would—Hey! Aren't you Swingin' Slim Simpson?"

Slim flashed one of his perfect smiles. "Why, yes I am," he said.

The waitress, a young red-haired woman with pale skin that was rapidly reddening, pressed her hand to her chest. "Oh, my beau and I are going to your concert tomorrow! We just love you, Mr. Simpson. We made sure to go stand in line the minute tickets went on sale so we wouldn't miss out!" she said.

"That's terrific," Slim said. "I'm happy to hear it.

I wonder if I might get a mug of your hot chocolate. Miss Kittredge's smells so good, and it would be just the right thing to warm up our interview."

"Interview?" the waitress asked.

"For the newspaper, yes," Slim said.

The waitress gave Kit a look of surprise and newfound respect. Kit couldn't help feeling triumphant.

"One hot chocolate coming up!" the waitress said, speeding off toward the kitchen.

"Thanks again for meeting me," Kit said gratefully.

She opened her notebook in front of her. The first question about why he'd wanted to become a musician suddenly looked silly. And she wanted to jump right in and ask about his past in Cincinnati, but she had learned that the best way to get an interviewee to open up was to start out with simple and impersonal questions.

"You're touring the entire country with your

band," Kit said. "That's a lot of traveling. Is it fun, or does it get really tiring after a while?"

Slim nodded as Kit spoke, which made her feel as if she'd asked a good question.

"We'll do twenty states in four months. That's a lot of traveling—and a lot of work. Sometimes we get great digs, but we spend lots of nights in real fleabag hotels too. But getting out there, getting face-to-face with the people who love swing, well, there's nothing better!"

Kit wrote quickly but carefully. She knew it was important that she get down every sentence just as Slim had spoken it. She was about to go right on to the third question on her list when something Slim had said made her change her mind.

"I know that the kind of jazz that's popular now, which you and your band play, is called swing," Kit said. "Can you talk a little about what swing actually is? What it means?"

"Great question," Slim said. Kit flushed with

pleasure and felt her confidence soar.

"Swing. What is it? Well, you sock it on the downbeat and punch it on the offbeat, and never ever play it straight," Slim declared.

Kit's mind went completely blank, her confidence suddenly gone. She had absolutely no idea what Slim meant.

If you don't understand him, how will your readers? Kit told herself. *Ask the questions they would want to ask.*

"I'm afraid I don't understand," Kit said.

Slim laughed. "That's why it's such a great question! I'm not sure anyone really understands. Swing just is what it is—a musical feeling—how do you put that into words? Swing is powerful because it's got the push of the big brass—all those trumpets and trombones and saxophones. But swing is also light because the rhythm is so lilting, and always off center. Nothing is ever plain old beats, like *ta ta ta ta.* Swing dances around every beat—some notes get held much longer, and some get rushed through or sped up or run around. But you know you're playing it right when people's feet start tapping. Swing is magic—it makes people move. It bounces! It's jazz on springs."

Kit wrote as fast as she could, her pencil moving furiously across the paper. The way Slim described it, she almost *did* understand what he meant.

Suddenly, a blur of movement outside the window caught Kit's eye, and she looked up in time to see Trixie with her big hat hugged to her chest, running away from the theater. Had something happened to her?

This is an interview and I have to stay focused, Kit reminded herself, turning back to her list of questions. Now that Slim was warmed up, she decided, maybe he would be willing to answer some more personal questions.

"It was very exciting to learn that a real swing band was going to play at the Burns Theater," Kit continued. "The tickets sold out in one day. I'm sure our readers are curious how a band that's playing the biggest clubs in twenty states ended up booking a night in our little theater."

Slim looked out the window. "Maybe I was indulging in a little walk down memory lane," he said.

Kit listened quietly, hoping that Slim would reveal some information that might bring her closer to figuring out who had put the message on the marquee.

"You know," Slim continued, "I grew up in this neighborhood—in a little house not far from here, actually. I used to go to the Burns Theater as a kid, to catch whatever show was there."

Now was her chance. Kit swallowed her nervousness and sat a little taller. "Do you still know anybody in Cincinnati?"

Slim paused, studying Kit's face. "You're a smart kid, Kit. How old are you? About twelve?"

Kit nodded.

"That's a great age," Slim said. "Young enough to still be a kid, but old enough to be doing great things, like you are. You remind me of . . . well, that's silly. But I'm glad we got the chance to talk."

Kit nodded. She was disappointed that he hadn't answered her question, but knew that she mustn't press the issue. So she just smiled and took the last sip of her hot chocolate.

"I finished mine too," Slim laughed. Then he looked at his watch and whistled. "Oh boy, I'd better get moving. I've got to get that rehearsal started. Are you going to listen in?"

"Of course, if it's still all right with you," Kit said.

"Sure thing."

Then Kit thought of Trixie. She had looked upset when she ran by. Did she think she'd been stood up?

"Mr. Simpson, I have a friend helping me with my article. Do you think it would be okay if she came to the rehearsal too?" Kit knew that Trixie would love the chance to watch Slim and his band rehearse.

"Sure, bring her along. Just make sure your friend understands she needs to stay very quiet, okay?"

Kit nodded solemnly. "She's actually a huge fan of yours," she told Slim. "She knows way more about jazz than I do. I'm sure she'll behave perfectly."

"Then you choose your friends wisely," Slim said, smiling. "Now, I really do have to get going." He placed a dollar on the table. "See you at rehearsal."

chapter 8

Topsy-Turvy

KIT LEFT THE coffee shop at a sprint. She wanted to find Trixie, but she was determined not to miss too much of Slim's rehearsal. First she checked the park, where she and Trixie had met, but Trixie was nowhere to be seen. Then she remembered that Trixie had said she lived in an apartment on Braverman Avenue. *Who knows if she's there,* thought Kit. *But it's worth a try. I have to find her!*

After running for four blocks, Kit was breathing heavily. The Braverman Arms was the only apartment building on Braverman Avenue—the rest of the buildings were townhouses or shops. It wasn't a large building—there were just two apartments on the ground floor. The main door was open, so Kit walked into the tiny lobby. Ahead lay a staircase, and on each side of that a door.

No point checking the mailboxes, since I don't know Trixie's last name, Kit decided. She walked to the door on the right and rang the doorbell. Maybe one of Trixie's neighbors would be able to point her to the right apartment. After a moment she heard footsteps, and the door, secured by a chain, opened a crack.

"Trixie!" Kit exclaimed with delight. "I found you!"

Trixie drew back. "What are you doing? Why did you come here?" she asked, her voice tight and strange.

"W-what do you mean?" Kit stuttered, bewildered by Trixie's chilliness.

"Where were you?" Trixie said, looking like she was about to cry.

"I'm sorry that I didn't show up," Kit said. "I was afraid you might be upset, and that's why I came looking for you. But I think you'll understand when I tell you where I was!" She paused, a little dramatically, to give Trixie the chance to push her for details. But Trixie just stood there, with an odd expression on her face.

"Okay, well . . . yesterday after you took off, I actually got a chance to meet Slim Simpson! I asked him if he'd give me an interview, and he said yes! That's what I was doing when I was supposed to be meeting you—interviewing him at the coffee shop just down the street. I saw you run by, but I couldn't interrupt Slim."

"You saw me?" Trixie said, suddenly looking very nervous.

"I did—and you looked so upset, I felt just terrible. So the minute we were finished, I rushed over here to find you and explain. So you're not mad, are you?"

A look of relief crossed Trixie's face, but Kit noticed that her friend still didn't open the door all the way or invite her inside.

"No, of course not," Trixie replied. "I mean,

that's great that you got your interview, Kit."

"I haven't even told you the best part," said Kit. "Slim invited me to sit in on the rehearsal today—and he said you could come, too!"

"Y-you told him about me?" Trixie asked.

"Sure did!"

Trixie bit her lip. "What exactly did you tell him?"

"I told him that I had a friend helping me with the article, that's all. Why?"

"No reason," Trixie said quickly, shaking her head for emphasis. "But I'm sorry, Kit—I can't come to the rehearsal."

"But why not? You're a huge fan, and you don't have a ticket to the show, so you can come right now and hear him play for free!" Kit pressed. "A private show just for us!"

"I just can't," Trixie said, casting a quick glance over her shoulder. She leaned closer to Kit. "My mother would be angry. I can't explain right now—she's in the kitchen. I really appreciate it, Kit, but you really should go now. Okay?"

Trixie's face was tight with anxiety. Whatever was going on between her and her mother, Kit did not want to make it worse, so she swallowed her disappointment. "I understand," she said quietly. "Well, I've got to get back to the theater. I'll tell you all about it tomorrow, okay?"

Trixie glanced over her shoulder again.

"Sure. Okay," she whispered. "Have fun, Kit." And with that she pushed the door shut.

That was odd, Kit thought. But she didn't have time to give it another thought. If she ran a little faster, she figured she could be back to the theater in ten minutes—just in time to catch most of Slim's rehearsal.

Kit was panting when she arrived at the theater, and she paused to catch her breath before she entered from the lobby. But when she stepped inside, she found that the theater was anything but silent.

Onstage, Dex and Slim seemed to be having some kind of argument. A cluster of musicians were gathered around them, each talking over the others. Hootie Shay, the baritone sax player, was barreling up the aisle at full speed. He slowed down when he saw Kit.

"Did you see anyone go through that lobby?" he asked her sharply.

"What?" Kit asked.

"I'm asking if you saw anyone leaving the theater just now."

"I . . . no, I didn't," Kit said.

"Darn," Hootie said. "Anyone out there working? That stagehand, the little bald guy with the plaid cap. I saw him in the lobby earlier—is he still there?"

"Graham's assistant?" Kit asked. "No, I didn't see him."

"I see," Hootie said, wringing his hands and looking back at the stage, where Slim stood, his face turning redder by the second.

"Mr. Shay? May I ask what's going on?" Kit asked timidly.

The saxophone player turned back to Kit. His expression softened slightly. "Sorry, kid, I didn't mean to be rude. We're in the middle of a situation here. Looks like somebody from the outside got into the theater while we were doing some cleanup onstage. Slim stashed his things in the greenroom while he want to meet a reporter for an interview. When he got back, he asked me to go get his trumpet for him. I went to get it from the greenroom, and the trumpet case was empty. Somebody stole Slim's trumpet."

Kit stared at Hootie, horrified. *Stolen?* And then she realized: *Slim was with* me *when his trumpet was stolen.*

Hootie rubbed his forehead. "Slim wanted

us to make darn sure we turned this place upside down before we called the cops, in case someone moved it by accident or something. But that trumpet is one in a million. No one picks it up and sticks it somewhere by accident. I'm telling you, it's gone."

"So you'll be calling the police?" Kit asked.

"Slim's not ready to do that. He's got it in his head that if the cops come in, he'll never see that trumpet again. Whoever snatched it probably hasn't gone far yet, but if a bunch of police show up at the theater, the thief will hotfoot it out of town. Slim wants to see what happens—if anyone calls the theater or leaves a ransom note."

"You mean he thinks someone might have kidnapped the trumpet for ransom?" Kit asked. She suddenly wondered if Slim thought that somebody was out to hurt him. Was that why he had avoided her question about knowing anybody in Cincinnati?

Hootie shrugged. "The way he figures it, who-ever took that trumpet knows what he has. And anyone who knows trumpets is aware that there isn't another King Liberty Silver Tone like that one in the world. Too hot to sell, too hot to keep. The guy may be somewhere nearby, waiting for a chance to make contact. He'll know Slim might be willing to deal—but only if there are no cops around."

Kit bit her lip. "If he hasn't found it by tomorrow night, does he have a backup trumpet? Or could he borrow someone else's?"

Hootie sighed heavily. "Kid, that trumpet *is* Slim. It's his sound. His trademark. If that trumpet doesn't turn up, I don't think there's going to be any concert tomorrow night. He'll cancel the whole rest of the tour."

"Oh," Kit said, pressing one hand to her stom-ach. She felt as if she might be sick.

"Hey, it's not your fault," Hootie said gently. "But Slim's gonna be in a real temper. Might be best for you to clear out."

"I understand," she said.

Just then the lobby door opened and in walked the man with the plaid cap.

"Ah, there you are," Hootie said. "We need all hands on deck, Mr.—"

"Montague," the man said, giving a dramatic bow. "Thomas Montague, at your service."

Hootie turned to Kit and nodded toward the door. "You go on home, Kit. We've got everything covered here."

Kit walked home in a daze. Slim's trumpet stolen! The show possibly canceled!

"Everything's gone topsy-turvy," Kit murmured as she started up the walkway to her house.

"Who ya talking to?" came a voice from right behind Kit.

Kit gave a little shriek and whirled around.

"Stirling, you scared me half to death!"

"Sorry," he said with a sheepish grin. "So what's gone topsy-turvy?"

Kit sighed and sat down on the steps by the front door. "I don't even know where to start."

Stirling plopped down next to her. "Well, how about with the interview—how'd it go?"

"Oh, that," Kit said distractedly.

"Wait, I thought this was supposed to be the big career break you've been waiting for! What happened—did he stand you up?"

"No, he showed up," Kit said, pulling her notebook out of her bag and staring at it. "The interview went fine. But then when I got to the theater for rehearsal, it was pandemonium. Apparently someone got into the greenroom and *stole* Slim's trumpet."

Stirling whistled. "That's big-time. Did the cops come?"

"Not yet," Kit said. "And you have to promise

not to tell anyone. Hootie, he's one of the musicians, told me that Slim thinks his best chance at getting the trumpet back is not getting the police involved right away. He thinks the thief might try to hold it for ransom."

"Huh," Stirling said. "But what if it was the same person who put the message up on the marquee . . . and tore the poster . . . and wrote that letter to the editor—someone who's out to get Slim for revenge, or some other personal reason?"

"I don't know what to think," Kit answered. "All I know is, Hootie says if Slim doesn't get his trumpet back, the show will be canceled."

"Whoa," Stirling said. "That would sure be bad news for Miss Burns—and for you, Kit."

"I know. I wish I could figure out why someone would do this."

Stirling perked up. "I might have something that could give you some answers! Hang on—I'll be right back."

While she waited for Stirling, Kit sat very still, racking her brain. The first question to answer was *Who had access to the greenroom?*

Miss Burns, of course. But there was no reason for Miss Burns to steal the very trumpet that was going to bring in a full house of paying customers.

Graham. Kit winced at the thought. She'd already suspected him in the cash box theft in the theater that summer. But he'd been completely innocent then, and Kit had to admit that, just like Miss Burns, he was an unlikely suspect now.

There was one more person with access to the greenroom, Kit realized—*Graham's assistant*, the man with the plaid cap. But again, why would he do all those horrible things?

And then there's Dex. He could have a motive to steal the trumpet; if Slim were to cancel his performance, Dex could step in and be the star of the entire show.

And what about the rest of Slim's band—and his

entire crew? They could all be possible culprits, but why would any of them steal the trumpet *now* when they had had access to it since the start of Slim's tour? It simply didn't make any sense.

Who else had been around the theater, had access, and had some connection to the concert? Kit gasped when a familiar name popped into her head: *Trixie.*

chapter 9

A Hard Discovery

KIT'S CHEEKS TURNED hot. It felt disloyal to even consider that Trixie could be a suspect. But Kit couldn't ignore the fact that Trixie had been in or near the theater every time Kit had encountered an act of vandalism. Kit had seen her outside the theater shortly after she had come across the damaged display and torn poster. Trixie had left so suddenly when Slim had arrived in the theater that first day, and then a short time later Kit had discovered the threatening message on the marquee. And Trixie had been at the theater this afternoon, around the time that the trumpet had been stolen.

Just then Stirling came through the front door, triumphantly holding up a large envelope.

"When I went to return the extra papers from

my route today, I stopped by the archive office
to see if they had anything on Slim Simpson. Here's
what they gave me," he said, handing it to Kit.

Kit cleared her throat, hoping to hide the wobble
in her voice. "Wow, Stirling, thanks," Kit said.

"You're welcome," Stirling said, seeming not to
notice that Kit's disposition had changed. "But I've
got to take it back tomorrow. And be really careful.
The clippings are fragile."

"I'll be really careful," Kit said, peaking at the
yellowing old newspaper clippings inside.

She had managed to do no more than open the
envelope when she heard Mrs. Howard inside the
house, calling Stirling's name.

Stirling rolled his eyes. "Guess I'd better go see
what she wants. I hope you find something in that
envelope that helps."

"I do too, Stirling," Kit said.

She followed him inside and bounded up the
stairs to her attic room. She sat on her bed with the

large envelope lying in front of her.

There's got to be something in here, Kit thought.

There were at least twenty articles in the envelope. Kit began to leaf through the faded yellow newspaper clippings. Most of them were short, announcing some new career first of Slim's and reminding readers that he was a hometown boy.

But one of them was a profile on Slim from the Sunday edition, a longer and more detailed story.

Kit scanned through the article, her finger stopping on the heading "Home Life." She began to read, but stopped when a line caught her eye. "He married his high school sweetheart, Daphne Selbourne, in 1921, and they had a child," she read aloud.

Kit frowned. Slim had never mentioned his family in their interview. She scanned back through her notes from the interview to see if Slim had even hinted about a family. *Are they still here in Cincinnati?* she wondered. *Or did they follow him to Chicago?* She would have to chase down these answers for her article. *But there won't be any article if there isn't a concert,* Kit realized. Somehow she had to help Slim get his trumpet back.

The next morning was Saturday, the day of the concert. After Kit had eaten breakfast and finished her household chores, she slipped on a sweater and made her way over to Trixie's apartment. When she knocked, Trixie's mother answered the door.

"Hello, ma'am," Kit said politely. "My name is Kit, and I'm a friend of Trixie's. Is she home?"

"Yes," said Trixie's mother. "Please come in."

Kit stepped inside. The little hallway opened into a tiny living room.

"Trixie's room is the first door on the right," said her mother, pointing down the hallway. "She's been keeping to herself since breakfast. I'm sure she'll appreciate some company."

"Thank you," Kit said.

Kit hesitated at Trixie's door to gather herself, and then knocked.

"Come in," came a muffled reply. Kit opened the door and found Trixie lying on her bed, which was rumpled and piled high with scattered pillows and a bunched-up quilt.

Trixie looked up with a blank expression, and then did a double take.

"Kit?" she asked.

"Hi," Kit said, offering her friend a gentle smile.

"I—" Trixie looked around. "I'm sorry . . . it's just such a mess in here. I would have tidied up if I'd known you were coming." She yanked her pink-and-yellow bedspread up over the quilt and pillows.

"Oh, gosh, don't worry about that," Kit said, walking over to the bed. "My room gets really messy too sometimes." She sat down on the bed and opened her mouth to ask Trixie about the

trouble at the theater. Her elbow hit against something hard that was covered by the bedspread.

"Ouch," Kit said, rubbing her elbow. "What
in the world do you have under here?"

Trixie just stared at Kit, her face going pale.
Puzzled, Kit drew back the bedspread to see what
she had bumped into.

It was a shiny silver trumpet, its bell engraved
with four-leaf clovers.

Kit turned to face Trixie, her eyes wide with
disbelief.

"It was you?" Kit asked.

Trixie shook her head. "You don't understand,"
she whispered before bursting into tears.

"What is there to understand?" Kit exclaimed.
"Do you have any idea how much trouble this has
caused? Slim has threatened to cancel the show—
and I vouched for you to Miss Burns and Dex. Why
on earth did you steal it?"

"It isn't what you think!" Trixie whispered, tears

rolling down her cheeks. "I never meant to take it! Please, Kit, you've got to believe me."

Kit paused and bit the inside of her cheek. *I at least owe it to her to listen to what she has to say,* she decided. "Okay," she said calmly. "Why don't you tell me what happened, then."

Trixie took a deep, shuddering breath and nodded.

"When I was supposed to meet you at the theater," she said, "I got there right on time, but you weren't there. I started to worry I might have gotten the time mixed up, and I thought you might already be inside. The lobby door was locked, so I decided to go in through the stage door like that first time I went to the theater. It was propped open with a chair like before, so I went inside, but you weren't in the greenroom. Then I noticed the trumpet—Slim's King Liberty Silver Tone—just sitting there in its open case. It was so beautiful! I just wanted to hold it and see it up close. It was dark in the greenroom, so I carried the trumpet to the door so that I could see it in the sunlight. I stepped outside—but I forgot about the chair and accidentally walked right into it. It tipped over, and the door slammed shut. I tried the handle, but it was locked, and there I was standing outside still holding the trumpet! I was trying to figure out what I should do when I heard someone inside shouting, 'Where's Slim's trumpet?'"

"So you panicked?" Kit asked.

Trixie nodded. "All I could think was that no one would ever believe that I ended up outside the theater with that trumpet by accident, even though that's what really happened. So I just turned and ran and didn't stop running until I got home." Trixie rubbed her hand over a fat tear that was rolling down her cheek.

"Oh, Trixie," Kit said. "I can understand why you panicked. But would it have been so awful to bang on the stage door and tell the truth?"

"I couldn't do that!" Trixie cried. "What if Slim Simpson was the one who opened the door? What would he have thought of me, sneaking around with his trumpet?"

Kit squinted, trying to read the look in Trixie's eyes. She wanted to believe her friend—what Trixie was saying sounded believable. And if Trixie's story was true, it sounded like the missing trumpet wasn't connected to the other strange events at the theater—which would make Trixie innocent of those at least. The most important thing was to return the trumpet to Slim right away.

"There's only one way to fix this, Trixie," said Kit. "Let me take the trumpet back to Slim."

"I don't want you to get into trouble," Trixie argued. "How will you explain how you got your hands on that trumpet?"

Kit shrugged. "Hootie Shay told me if the trumpet was returned, no questions would be asked because Slim would be so relieved just to have it again. I'll tell him the truth—that the person who took it asked me to give it back. That's all I'll say."

"Slim might be furious with you!" Trixie said, but she handed Kit the trumpet. Kit felt its cool metal and its weight in her hands. She could see why Trixie had been so transfixed by it.

"I suppose he might be," Kit replied. "But what other choice do I have?"

chapter 10

Accused!

KIT HUGGED THE trumpet close to her chest and ran all the way to the theater. She burst into the lobby and pushed through the double doors into the theater, but it was empty—no musicians rehearsing, no stagehands painting music stands. An eerie silence filled the theater. She went back into the lobby and heard the sound of raised voices coming from Miss Burns's office.

"I'm telling you I can't do it. I'm not doing this show without that trumpet!"

Kit froze in her tracks, cradling the trumpet.

"Slim, the band stands to lose a lot of money over this, and so do I!" exclaimed another man.

The door to Miss Burns's office flew open and Slim stormed out, with Dex close behind him.

"I realize that, but I've just taken a major hit here," Slim was saying angrily. "I'm canceling the rest of the tour."

"I can't tell you how sorry I am!" came Miss Burns's voice; then she too came through the doorway. All three of them noticed Kit at the same time.

The world seemed to stop turning for a moment as Kit lifted the trumpet in both hands without uttering a word.

"It was you?" Dex cried.

"Kit!" exclaimed Miss Burns. "How did you . . . *where* did you—"

Slim, speechless, stepped toward Kit, taking the trumpet in his outstretched hands. He ran his hands over the bell gently, as if the instrument were a small animal that might be frightened.

"My trumpet," Slim whispered. But he didn't have the happy look on his face Kit was expecting. Instead, his expression darkened, and he fixed his eyes on Kit. "So who did your dirty work for you, kid?"

"W-what do you mean?" Kit asked, swallowing hard. Trixie had been afraid of this, but Kit had been certain he'd be relieved.

"Mr. Simpson," Miss Burns said, aghast, "you couldn't possibly believe Kit would—"

"What other explanation is there?" Slim snapped. "Kit and I had an appointment that required me to leave the theater, and while I was at that appointment, someone sneaked in and stole the trumpet. Clearly Kit was trying to distract me so that her accomplice could pull off the heist," Slim said, giving Kit a grim look.

Kit tried to say something, but a lump was forming in her throat and she felt like the air had been knocked out of her.

Slim continued to tear into her. "C'mon, kid. You wouldn't be the first reporter to cook up something to make a story more interesting, like that reporter who concocted the whole feud between me and Dex. I gotta say, I never thought a girl like you would stoop so low."

"I . . . I . . . " Kit stammered.

"Hey, Slim, lay off the poor kid," Dex interrupted. "You said there'd be no questions asked if the trumpet was returned. And here it is—where's the big news story in that? I think you're being too hard on her."

"I have to agree," stated Miss Burns. "With all due respect, Mr. Simpson, I have always found Kit to be honest and upright. Let's not accuse her without hearing what she has to say first."

Slim straightened his posture and rolled his shoulders back. "I'm sorry if I upset you, Miss Burns. I think I'd better go to the greenroom and cool down," he said. "Dex, you can let the others know we'll go on tonight, but I don't want to be bothered by anyone for the next hour." Slim strode past them, without giving Kit so much as a glance.

"Are you okay, Kit?" Dex asked. "Slim can be rough when he loses his temper."

Kit nodded, but she felt dangerously close to crying. "Um, I'm going to go get some air," she said, pushing the door to the street open before she even finished her sentence.

She heard Miss Burns call her name but pretended she hadn't. She raced across the street to the park and sat heavily on a wooden bench, her heart hammering.

I got Slim his trumpet back and protected Trixie like I promised, and now Slim thinks I was part of it! Kit burst into tears.

After a few minutes, she pulled a handkerchief from her pocket and wiped her face, sniffing a little. She knew that she ought to go back into the theater and talk to Miss Burns. *But I can't. I can't face any of them*, she thought miserably.

Would Slim decide he no longer wanted Kit's interview with him to be used in her story? Could he do that? Was it her responsibility as a reporter to ask him?

I should talk to Gibb, Kit thought. He'd placed so much trust in her when he'd given her this chance. And now the subject of her article had just accused her of stirring up trouble for her story. How could she tell Gibb that?

Kit knew that what had happened wasn't her fault. But she couldn't talk to Gibb about this—not yet. She knew there was more to the story.

Trixie had taken the trumpet, but Kit still didn't quite understand why her friend had run home with it. And Kit knew that someone had been vandalizing the theater, but she still had no idea who. *If I don't get to the bottom of this, the vandal might do something else—maybe even during Slim's concert tonight!* Kit thought. *And Slim will leave believing I had his trumpet stolen so that my newspaper story would be more dramatic. And what if Gibb believes him? I'll never be able to clear my name.*

Kit stood up, straightened her skirt, and smoothed her hair. She composed herself with a quiet breath, crossed the street, and marched back to the theater.

chapter 11

An Inside Job

DEX AND MISS Burns were still in the lobby. As Kit walked in the front door, Miss Burns turned and gave her a look of surprise and relief.

"Kit, we're so glad you've come back," Miss Burns said, placing a reassuring hand on Kit's shoulder.

"I didn't take the trumpet," Kit told her. "I only found it and brought it back."

Dex nodded. "We'll set things right between you and Slim once we sort out everything that still needs to get done before the show."

"Thanks, Dex," said Kit. Then she had a realization: Why would Dex help her clear her name if he was hoping to sabotage the concert himself? He couldn't be the culprit!

Just then, Graham walked into the lobby from the theater, interrupting Kit's thoughts. "There you are, Miss Burns," Graham said. "A few trucks just pulled into the alley by the stage door. One guy's got the programs for tonight and another has all the food and beverages for the concession stand. And the missing music stands just got here, too. Should we bring it all in through the stage door?"

"There goes Slim's hour of quiet," Dex said with a smile.

"Oh dear," Miss Burns said. "Graham, can you bring everything through the lobby instead?"

"Sure, I'll let the men outside know," said Graham, wiping his brow. "Whew, this is going to be an exhausting day. I could sure use a little help."

"What about your new assistant?" Miss Burns asked.

"You mean the bum who promised he'd help me out around here if I helped him fix up his porch, which I did?" Graham grumbled. "He never showed up. Sorry, Miss Burns. We've been so busy, I forgot to tell you."

Kit frowned. "What about Mr. Montague, the man with the plaid cap who helped you bring in the stage flats?" she asked. "Isn't he your assistant?"

"Mr. who?" asked Graham. "No, he's part of the band's crew."

Dex shook his head. "He isn't with us. I just assumed he worked for the theater."

"Nope, it's just me and Miss Burns here. My assistant didn't show." Graham looked at his watch. "Listen, I've gotta go tell the drivers to pull the trucks up front and load the stuff through this way."

As Graham left, Kit turned to Miss Burns. "If the man with the plaid cap isn't Graham's assistant, and he isn't with the band, then who is he?"

"You think he's connected to the trumpet theft?" Dex asked.

Kit shook her head. "The person who took the trumpet took it by accident." When Dex and Miss

Burns gave her puzzled looks, she added, "It's sort of a long story."

"Then let's not waste time worrying about it," Dex said.

"Unfortunately, I can't just ignore it," Miss Burns said. "We've had some odd acts of vandalism at the theater over the last few days. Small things—I'm almost tempted to say childish—a broken display case, a torn poster. And someone tampered with the letters on the marquee. I didn't say anything at the time because I felt it was a theater problem, not a concert problem. It wasn't until Slim's trumpet was stolen that I became very concerned. Kit, was the person who stole the trumpet responsible for the other things?"

Kit shook her head. "I really don't think so. Based on what I know, it doesn't make any sense that this person would want to cause any trouble for Slim."

"Cause trouble for Slim?" Dex asked, looking

surprised. "I don't think the guy has an enemy in the world. Except for me—according to a Chicago reporter with an overactive imagination. You really think someone here in Cincy is looking to settle an old score with Slim, or something like that?"

"No," Kit said suddenly. Dex and Miss Burns looked at her. "I think we've had it wrong. I did think someone might be targeting Slim. The poster for the show was torn apart, and the letters on the marquee were rearranged to say 'Slim go home,' or something like that. But now I don't think Slim himself was the real target, Miss Burns. I think the target is the concert."

"I'm afraid I'm not following you, Kit," Miss Burns said.

"Well, the acts of vandalism all took place outside the theater, but the one thing they have in common is Slim's concert. Now we've just realized that a stranger—this Mr. Montague— has been inside the theater on several occasions.

Whoever this man is, he knew enough about the theater to slip inside and blend in, as if he was counting on nobody asking him who he was."

Miss Burns still looked baffled. Dex was looking from Miss Burns to Kit, grinning as if he were watching an especially good performance unfold.

"So," Kit continued, "I'm trying to think of who might have been inside this theater before, and might have had something against this concert. Miss Burns, did you tell me that someone had booked the theater for this weekend, but his contract fell through?"

"Julian Steele," Miss Burns said, nodding. "He wanted the theater for the entire weekend," she added. "He'd been to some shows here and said it was perfect for him. He had some kind of solo show—he went on and on about it. He signed his contract but never paid the deposit. So when Slim's manager wanted to book this date, I jumped at it."

"Well, if the guy wasn't willing to pay up, why

would he have a beef with Slim?" Dex asked.

"Well, he wanted to do his show here, and now Slim's concert is happening instead," Kit replied. "Maybe he thinks Miss Burns dropped him because something flashier came along."

"Well, there's definitely no shortage of show business people with huge egos who think the world's out to get them," Dex said. "I'm with Kit—I'm thinking this could be our guy. We should at least talk to him. What's this Steele fellow look like?"

"We never actually met," Miss Burns said. "We only spoke on the phone."

Just then the lobby doors opened, and what looked like a parade of people came through. Graham and a large, heavyset man were carrying two stacks of music stands, and a boy not much older than Kit dragged a third one. Some men in white uniforms carried boxes of fresh food and beverages in glass bottles. Then a small man in a plaid cap shuffled in behind them, carrying a box.

Suddenly Kit thought of a way to test her hunch. "Mr. Steele!" she called loudly.

The man in the plaid cap stopped in the doorway to the auditorium. "Yes?" he asked. Then his face changed, and he dropped the box and rushed through the door.

"That's him! That's Steele!" Kit cried.

Dex raced after him. By the time Kit and Miss Burns went through the auditorium door, Steele was jumping over rows of seats, scrambling toward the stage. Dex was right behind him and catching up fast. He tackled the smaller man just as he reached the stage. As Dex yanked the little man to his feet, Slim walked out onstage looking irritated.

"What in Sam Hill is going on out here?" he thundered.

"We have an uninvited guest," Dex announced. "He's been hanging around for a few days, and up to no good. Isn't that right, Mr. Steele?"

"I have a perfect right to be here," the man said,
sniffing and brushing Dex's hands off him as
if they were bugs. "The theater is open to all."

"It's open to all ticket holders during a show,"
Miss Burns said.

"This was supposed to be *my* show!" Steele
snapped.

"You defaulted on the contract, and you were
given ample warning," Miss Burns said.

"I'm an actor, not a lawyer," the little man
said. "I didn't read any of that legal mumbo jumbo,
but I booked this theater—and then this smooth-
talking jazzman here came and took it right out
from under me!"

"Hey, is this the guy who stole my trumpet?"
Slim demanded.

"I didn't steal anything! What would I want
with an old trumpet? This is a *theater*. This is
a place for the actor and the dramatist, not for

dinner-jacketed dandies to play shiny instruments,"
Steele barked.

"But you *did* try to sabotage the show," Miss
Burns said. "You vandalized my theater—tampered
with the marquee and smashed the poster display."

Mr. Steele sneered. "You can't prove I've done
anything," he declared.

"We have all the proof we need in the contract
you filled out for Miss Burns," Kit blurted. "Once we
compare your handwriting to the anonymous letter
to the editor that you submitted to the *Herald* ... "
Kit's voice trailed off when she saw the confused
look on Miss Burns's face. "He was trying to damage the theater's reputation. I wanted to tell you, but
you were already so worried about everything else
that was happening, I—"

"Poppycock!" Steele snapped.

Kit glared at him. "Then why would you
introduce yourself to me and Hootie as Thomas
Montague? Clearly you were up to no good."

"Meaningless hypothesizing," he scoffed. "You can't prove anything! And frankly, it's beneath me to even stand in the same room as this . . . this *blowhorn*. I am leaving!"

Slim fixed Steele with a withering glare. "Get out of here, and stay out. If you come within ten blocks of this theater tonight, I'll have the cops lock you up before you can say William Shakespeare."

"With pleasure," Mr. Steele said. "I find this company most distasteful." He turned on his heel and swept away like royalty, hopping off the stage, pulling ineffectively on the fire door to open it, and then finally pushing it open and storming out.

"For a theater guy, he sure is a lousy actor," Dex observed, and everyone burst out laughing.

"What a dreadful man," Miss Burns said.

"Dollars to doughnuts he was fixing to pull some stunt tonight to sabotage the show," Dex said. "Thank heavens you figured it out, Kit."

Slim approached Kit and leaned down to look

her in the eye. "Well, then, Kit Kittredge, I owe you
a big thank-you—and a sincere apology. I still don't
quite understand how you managed to find my trumpet, but I suppose that's a story for another day."

Kit smiled. "As I told Miss Burns, it's a long
story. Let's just say that you have a very devoted fan
here in Cincinnati who wanted to get a little closer
to the great Swingin' Slim Simpson."

"Then maybe I can make it up to you by giving
you an extra ticket for the show," Slim offered.

"But the show is sold out!" Kit said.

"The bandleader always has a few tickets to
spare," Slim said. "I had been saving this last one
for—well, never mind. The ticket is yours, with
my thanks." He pulled the ticket out of his breast
pocket and handed it to Kit.

"Thank *you*, Mr. Simpson," said Kit as she took
the ticket. "Well, I'd better go—I know you have
a lot to do." She waved good-bye to Miss Burns
and the band members and headed out of the

auditorium through the lobby door.

"Finally, there you are!" said a familiar voice.

Kit looked around and saw with surprise that Stirling was sitting on the lobby floor under one of the windows. "Stirling, what are you doing here?"

He stood up. "When I brought that file on Slim back to work today, the archivist told me she'd found a few other clippings on him that were filed in photos. I thought you might be interested in this one."

He pulled a small envelope from his pocket and handed it to Kit. Inside was a quarter page cut from the paper with a photograph of a smiling, handsome Slim, a smiling young woman, and a little girl. Kit read the caption. "Mr. and Mrs. Stewart 'Slim' Simpson relaxing at home with their five-year-old daughter, Beatrice." Kit stared at the photo very hard. "Wait a minute . . . "

"What?" Stirling asked.

"What's a nickname for Beatrice?" Kit asked.

"I don't know. Bea, I guess."

"Maybe," Kit said, still staring at the picture. "Or maybe *Trixie*."

"Trixie?" Stirling asked. "What are you saying?"

Kit's eyes never left the photograph. "I'm saying I think that Trixie might be Slim Simpson's daughter."

chapter 12

Finding Beatrice

IT WOULD BE *too much of a coincidence*, Kit
thought as she turned onto Braverman Avenue.
Or would it? If Trixie really was Slim's daughter, it
could explain her reluctance to be caught returning
the trumpet. It would also explain why she knew
so much about him. But if Slim was her father,
why sneak around the theater? Trixie had said she
couldn't even get a ticket to the concert. But Slim
himself had tickets—like the one he'd just given Kit.
For every question that was answered, it seemed,
another one popped up.

There's only one way to find out, Kit told herself as
she walked through the front hall of the Braverman
Arms. She knocked on Trixie's door.

Trixie's mother looked surprised to see Kit for

the second time in one day, but she was just as polite and welcoming as she'd been the first time.

"Welcome back, Kit," she said. "Trixie's still in her room. Perhaps you can get her to talk about what has been bothering her all week."

Trixie was curled up on her bed. She sat up when Kit knocked and stepped inside.

"Did you give it to him?" she asked.

"Yes," Kit said. "Everything's fine. Well, at first it wasn't. But it is now." Kit sat down next to her friend. "I know you were telling the truth when you said you didn't mean to steal Slim's trumpet," Kit said. "But I'm not sure you told me the whole truth about why you were so scared to return it."

Trixie was silent. She looked curiously at Kit.

Kit didn't hesitate. "Trixie, is Slim Simpson your father?"

Trixie's mouth dropped open in shock.

"I'm right, aren't I?" Kit asked. "You're Beatrice."

Trixie looked at her in astonishment. "How

could you possibly know that?"

"I didn't absolutely know for sure until just now," Kit said. "But there were lots of little things that started to add up. Then a friend showed me this." Kit reached into her pocket and pulled out the newspaper photograph.

Trixie's eyes welled up with tears as she looked at the photo. "You mustn't tell anyone, Kit. Promise me. I don't want my mother to know I've been hanging around the theater. It would upset her terribly. Please don't say anything."

"If you don't want me to, of course I won't," Kit said. "I promise. But I don't understand, Trixie. You know so much about Slim and his career and his music. You sneaked into the theater just to catch a glimpse of him. But if he's your father, why wouldn't you just talk to him?"

Trixie's eyes brimmed with tears again, and she hung her head. "I wasn't sure what he'd do," she said. "Why would he even want to see me? He's never wanted to before—he never wanted me at all!"

"Trixie, I'm sure that isn't true!" Kit exclaimed. "How can you say such a thing?"

"Because it *is* true!" Trixie whispered. "If he cared even a little about me, why just leave and never even ask how I was?"

Kit didn't know what to say. "I'm sorry," was all she could come up with.

"You can't imagine what it's like when people are all excited that Slim Simpson is coming to town. I want to stand up and shout, 'That's my father!' What did I ever do that made him never want to see me again? How could he go all those years without even sending me a letter?"

"He did," said a voice from the doorway.

Kit and Trixie both jumped a little. Neither of them had noticed Trixie's mother opening the door.

"What—what do you mean?" Trixie stuttered.

"I'm sorry. I didn't mean to eavesdrop, but when I heard—" She dropped her head and sighed.

"Trixie, your father did write to you, when we still lived in our old apartment. I marked his letters 'return to sender.' When we moved here they were forwarded for a while, but they didn't come as often. When they did arrive, I sent them back. I wanted him to know they were being returned, so he'd know I was the one preventing you from responding. I suppose he gave up eventually."

"But why didn't you let me see his letters?" Trixie asked.

Trixie's mother leaned against the doorjamb. "I don't know," she said. "I used to know. I used to feel certain that I was doing the right thing. You were heartbroken when he left. You kept asking me over and over again why, why did he leave, what had you done wrong? You cried yourself to sleep every night. It was devastating to watch you go through that, Trix. There was no way to help you understand that he chose music over his family, because he couldn't have them both without neglecting one. It took so long for you to start feeling better. So long for you to sleep through the night again, and be happy. When that first letter came, I just couldn't bring myself to show it to you. I felt like you'd just begun to accept that life would be okay with just the two of us. I didn't want him pushing in on that. Then one day another letter came, and I sent that one back, too. And I just kept on doing it."

"Is that why you wouldn't even talk about him?" Trixie asked. "Whenever I asked, you'd just say 'What's done is done' and change the subject."

"I thought I was doing the right thing," Trixie's mother said again. "But now I'm not so sure. When I heard he was coming to town, I was afraid something like this would happen. I know you have his record albums. I know you collect the magazines that he's in. And I know you hide them from me because you don't want to upset me. You shouldn't have had to make that choice. You shouldn't have to hide things, especially about your own father. Even though he left us, I shouldn't have kept you from him." She blotted her eyes with a handkerchief. "I'm so sorry, Trixie."

Trixie got up and rushed over to her mother, hugging her tightly. "I know it's been hard for you doing everything by yourself, taking care of me, without anyone to help you."

"I wouldn't trade a second of it," Trixie's mother said fiercely. "And honestly, Trix, if there was a way for you to see your father now, even if there was just money for a ticket to see him play, I'd want you to see him. I really would."

Kit cleared her throat. She was afraid to say anything at all in the midst of this very delicate moment.

But Trixie had turned and was looking at her. "What is it?"

"Well," Kit said, "if it's okay with your mom, I could help with that." She turned to Trixie's mother and explained that she had been writing an article about Slim and his band and had gotten to know him a little. "Anyway, I helped him solve a problem today, and he gave me one of his own tickets to thank me. I came here to give it to Trixie, so she could come to the show tonight."

Trixie turned to look at her mother, whose eyes were filling with tears. She nodded tightly and squeezed Trixie's hand.

"That's a lovely invitation. You go, Beatrice. Go and see your father."

chapter 13

A Happy Reunion

KIT'S DAD STOOD near the front door, tug-
ging at his tie.

"And this trumpet player Dex just tackled Steele
right there? Honestly, Kit, if you weren't my own
daughter I'd have to wonder if you were making
some of this up! Say, is my tie straight?"

Kit peeked at the clock as her mother helped
Dad straighten his tie, and then checked her own
reflection in the mirror. Her navy blue dress looked
brand-new, though it wasn't. Her mother had
washed and ironed it so beautifully that even the
white collar was spotless. With her newly darned
white kneesocks and her just-polished Mary Janes,
Kit felt perfectly dressed for a night at the theater.

"It does sound like something right out of

a novel," Kit agreed. "But it's true, every word of it. We should go now, if we don't want to be late."

"Have a wonderful time, you two," Mother said.

"We'll tell you all about it," Kit promised.

"With any luck, you'll be reading all about it when Kit's article is published in the newspaper!" said Dad.

"*If* it's published," Kit corrected. "Dad, we really have to go!"

Mother walked them to the door and stood waving as Kit skipped happily down the walk with her father at her side. Dad smiled as Kit chattered happily about Slim and Dex and Hootie and Lady Deedles. She didn't stop talking until they were across the street from the theater, where a crowd was already gathered waiting to get inside.

"Oh, and there's Trixie!" Kit exclaimed happily. "Trix!" Kit called.

"I'm going to get us a place in line," Dad told her. "Go and get your friend, Kit. Then meet me in line."

"Thanks, Dad." Kit darted through the crowd. "Trixie, over here!"

Trixie spun around when she heard her name. Her dark hair was curled into soft ringlets. She was wearing a green dress with puffed sleeves, and patent leather shoes that looked like they'd just been shined.

"Oh, you look so pretty!" Kit exclaimed.

"So do you," Trixie said. "I can't believe I'm really here!"

Kit slipped her arm through Trixie's. "I'm so glad," she said. "Will you wait right here for me? I just need to let Miss Burns know something I forgot before. I'll be back in a jiffy."

"Sure," Trixie said.

Kit dashed into the lobby. Miss Burns was standing out front by the box office wiping a spot on the counter with a rag. "The house isn't open quite yet—" she murmured before she looked up. "Oh, Kit! Don't you look lovely!"

"Thank you!" Kit said. "Could you get a message to Slim before the show?"

Miss Burns looked at the clock on the wall and nodded. "Sure. What is it?"

"Just tell him that Kit says to look for Beatrice tonight."

"Look for Beatrice tonight?"

Kit nodded.

"Well, that's all very mysterious, Kit, but I'll be happy to pass along your message. I'll do it right now before we open the house and let the audience in."

"Thank you!" Kit called, hurrying back outside.

Kit's and Trixie's front-row seats were so close to the stage they could almost see the brushstrokes in the paint on the music stands. There was not an empty seat in the house. As the auditorium lights dimmed and an excited hush came over the crowd,

Kit turned around and waved at her father, who sat a few rows back. He had swapped tickets with Trixie so that the girls could sit together. He grinned and waved back, and then pointed at the stage. Dizzy Dex and Lady Deedles had just stepped onto the stage, and the audience cheered like mad.

Dex took in the crowd's admiration for a moment and then signaled for quiet. He put his trumpet to his lips and began to play the tune that Kit had heard when she'd found him playing alone on the stage just a few days ago. Lady Deedles joined in on the piano, adding a bass beat with her left hand and a harmony with her right. The crowd vibrated with energy as the band played a couple more songs. Then Dex smiled at the crowd and began to speak.

"When you open for a guy like Slim Simpson, you gotta know not to overstay your welcome. So if Lady Deedles doesn't mind, I'm just gonna warm you folks up with one of my favorite tunes, 'It's Only a Paper Moon,' while the fellas come onstage."

Lady Deedles began to play a series of lively chords, as if it were no effort at all. Her blonde hair was swept up into an elegant French twist, and the gleaming jewels around her neck sparkled against her black dress like stars in the night. As Dex started to play, Slim's musicians began to file onstage, each dressed in a white dinner jacket and black trousers. They took their seats at their music stands, their instruments gleaming in the stage lights. Everything looked absolutely perfect.

Dex began hamming it up as he played, his trumpet pointed toward the floor one moment and the next straight up in the air. As each musician took his seat, he joined in on his own instrument. The *wah-wah* of trombones joined the deep growl and hum of saxophones, the *doop-doop-doop* of the upright bass, and the powerful beat of the drums. Suddenly Dex let his trumpet drop down by his side, grinning mischievously as the tune he had been playing continued, clearly carried by another trumpet player. Dex gave a deep bow and a dramatic outward salute, and in strolled Slim Simpson, playing the final bars of "Paper Moon."

"It's Slim!" Kit cried, momentarily forgetting she was in a theater. But it didn't matter, because scores of other people shouted the same thing simultaneously, and the sound of applause erupted like a clap of thunder.

Slim waved to the audience and blew a kiss to Lady Deedles.

I can hardly believe I sat and interviewed him over hot chocolate, Kit thought, as Slim scanned the audience and smiled his dazzling smile. He wore the same white dinner jacket as his musicians, except he had a red carnation in his lapel. His hair was slicked back and his eyes shone. Maybe it was just the bright lights, but Kit thought Slim seemed to be glowing.

"Doesn't he look like a movie star?" Trixie whispered.

"He definitely does," Kit agreed.

"Thank you!" Slim said. "Thank you, Cincinnati—I am very, very happy to be here with you all tonight. I hope you're ready to swing!"

The audience clapped and whistled again. Kit nudged Trixie and giggled. It was funny to hear grown-ups so loud and excited, like kids at a circus.

"We've got some great numbers to share with you folks. But before we get started, I want to thank everyone at the Burns Theater for all the help you've given us over the last few days. I'm pretty sure the band and I were a lot more trouble than Miss Burns bargained for. I'm grateful for every show I get to play, but this one tonight is especially important to me. This isn't just another stop on the tour for me. I was born and raised in this part of Cincinnati, and tonight, I've come home." Slim paused. "Cincinnati has a special place in my heart, and I've made some great new friends while I've been here."

"He means you!" Trixie whispered, and sure

enough, Slim was looking straight at Kit. When he saw that she was looking back, he winked at her.

"So I always . . . " Slim's voice trailed off. He was still staring at the front row, but not at Kit.

He sees Trixie, Kit realized. *Miss Burns gave him my message.*

"I . . . uh, wow, sorry, folks, I got a little starry-eyed under these hot theater lights," Slim said as the audience chuckled.

As if on cue, Graham appeared onstage, a glass of water in one hand. He handed it to Slim and hurried offstage. Slim took a long drink from the glass. When he finished drinking, he looked back at Kit.

Holding Slim's gaze, Kit leaned her head a little toward Trixie and nodded. For a moment, that smooth, composed expression left Slim's face, replaced by something between sadness and relief. Then he quickly regained his composure.

"Folks, I loved growing up here, but that's not what makes this city the most important one in the world to me. No, it's because my beautiful daughter, Beatrice, lives here. She's the real reason I wanted to play at the Burns Theater. I've played gigs all over the country, but never one with my daughter in the audience. I have reason to believe that she might be here in the audience tonight," Slim said, looking straight at Trixie. "Beatrice has loved jazz ever since she was a baby. Every time I pick up a trumpet, I think of her. I hope she knows how proud I am to be her dad."

Kit peeked at Trixie, who sat frozen, her mouth open in a small *o*, her eyes on her father.

"If you are here, sweetheart, maybe you'd make your old dad's night by coming up here for a moment."

The audience broke into applause again, cheering.

"I don't know if I can," Trixie said, turning to Kit, her eyes wide with panic.

"Yes, you can! Just walk up those steps!" Kit

urged. "Oh, think of it, Trixie. He came back here for *you*! Go up there with him. You'll remember this night for the rest of your life!"

Trixie stood up, smoothed her dress, and walked up the stairs to her father. Kit felt tears spring to her eyes as Slim enveloped his daughter in a powerful hug. Everyone cheered, even Slim's musicians.

Slim leaned close, speaking quietly to Trixie. Her smile grew wide. They looked so much alike standing side by side; Kit couldn't believe she hadn't noticed that from the beginning.

"Okay, let's play some music!" Slim called over his shoulder to his band. "The first tune's for you, sweetheart. Anything you want to hear, just name it." He tilted down the microphone to Trixie's height, and she blushed nervously.

"How about 'Heebie Jeebies'?" Trixie asked.

"'Heebie Jeebies' it is! All right, boys, you heard the little lady, let's play it in C, and keep it hot!

Count us in, Boogie-Woogie!"

Trixie skipped back down the stairs and slid into her seat next to Kit as the music started.

"Did that just happen?" Trixie asked, her eyes shining.

"Yes, it really did!" Kit answered, beaming back at her friend.

"It feels like a dream," Trixie murmured.

Horns and saxes swayed in unison as the upright-bass player twirled his enormous fiddle. Slim conducted with one hand, then played a trumpet solo that zoomed from giddy squeals to brassy growls. Kit could feel the vibration of the music zinging through her. When she looked down, she was surprised to realize she'd been stamping her foot in time to the music. She remembered something Slim had said in their interview, when he said it was difficult to describe swing in words.

You know you're playing it right when people's feet start tapping. It's jazz on springs.

Kit laughed out loud and let her foot keep right on tapping. Now she understood what Slim meant. She knew the feeling.

This was swing.

chapter 14

A Dream
Come True

AND THERE IT was. Kit's finished article. She had spent all of Sunday writing and rushed home after school the next day to add the finishing touches. Finally, she was satisfied.

"I think I've got it," Kit said, pulling a sheet of paper from her typewriter. "What do you two think about this for a closing paragraph?"

Trixie, who was sitting on Kit's bed, sat up expectantly. Stirling was lounging on the floor with his eyes closed, but he said, "Go ahead. I'm listening."

Kit cleared her throat and began to read. The last part of her story was her favorite:

The crowd was already on its feet midway through the finale, and the floor seemed to vibrate when the horn section let loose. There was time for one last solo from Slim—blazing through the notes so fast you had to wonder how he found time to take a breath. The audience was caught up in the joy of the music—everywhere hands were clapping, feet were stomping, and heads were bobbing to the beat. When it was over, the standing ovation lasted for more than five minutes. It will be a long time before those lucky enough to hear Swingin' Slim Simpson and his band at the Burns Theater will stop talking about the night swing came to Cincinnati—and a father and daughter were reunited onstage.

"Wow," Trixie said after a moment. "Kit, that's really good."

Stirling sat up. "I agree," he said. "I think that ending is aces."

"Really?" Kit asked. "You're not just saying so to be nice?"

"Kit, we're your friends," Stirling said. "We don't need to be nice."

Kit burst out laughing, and Trixie started to laugh too.

"That didn't come out the way I meant it to," Stirling said.

"I know exactly what you mean," Kit said. "So it's done, then. I'll put it in an envelope and drop it by Gibb's office. I did tell him he'd have it on Monday before five o'clock, and it's almost four already."

Kit placed the page in her hand on top of several others, and then folded the pages neatly. Her hands shook slightly as she slid the pages into a brown paper envelope. No one could imagine how badly she wanted this piece to be published.

"I'll come with you," Trixie said.

"Me too," Stirling said, standing up.

"Thanks," Kit said. "I *am* really nervous. Having you two along will distract me."

The sun was bright outside, but the day was chilly and a few leaves were just beginning to turn, their edges bright red and deep yellow.

"Isn't life amazing sometimes?" Trixie asked as they walked shoulder to shoulder down the sidewalk. "Just think, Kit. A week ago, you and I had never met, and I thought I was never going to see my father again!"

"That *is* amazing," Kit agreed. "And it already feels like the concert was ages ago, but it was only yesterday. I'm sorry Slim had to leave so soon."

"I know, but they have a gig tomorrow night in Saint Louis. That's a long drive. Besides, he said he'd come back to visit after the tour ends in a couple of months."

"I think it would be cool to ride across the country in a bus full of jazzmen," Stirling declared.

"And I love their names. I want a jazz name. What do you think mine would be?"

"Stirling Ding-a-Ling Howard," Kit teased.

Stirling gave Kit a playful nudge.

"Not a silly name, a *real* one," Stirling said.

"Lots of their names are silly," Trixie said. "Like Jelly Roll Morton."

"Well, I want a royal name, like Count Basie or Duke Ellington," Stirling said.

Kit laughed. "How about King Stirling?"

"King's already taken," Trixie said. "Paul Whiteman's called the King of Jazz."

"Boy, Kit wasn't kidding—you do know a lot about jazz," Stirling said.

Kit stopped. "Well, this is it," she said, pointing at the red brick building. "Cincinnati Register" was painted in gold on the glass double doors. She had started to pull the heavy door when someone inside pushed it open. Kit recognized Jimmy Lake, one of the boys who worked in the newspaper's mailroom.

"Hi, Jimmy," she said. "I was just stopping by to drop something off for Gibb."

"He's about to leave for the day, so I'll take it right up for you," Jimmy offered.

"Oh, would you?" Kit said, handing him her story. She was glad to avoid going into the news-room. If Stirling and Trixie knew she felt practically sick with nerves, it would make it that much harder if Gibb turned down her article. She couldn't bear them feeling sorry for her.

"Sure thing, Kit," Jimmy said. He waved the envelope over his shoulder as the glass door swung shut behind him.

As they walked home, Stirling and Trixie chat-tered, but Kit was lost in thought. Watching the two of them talk and laugh together, she smiled. It always felt good when a new friend and an old friend liked each other. *And who would have thought I'd ever consider Stirling an old friend*, Kit thought. *It was just a year ago that Mother decided to take in boarders, and I thought home would never feel like home again. Then Stirling moved in, and now he's become a good friend.*

A person could never really know how something would turn out, Kit realized. And Slim Simpson's concert was no exception. She had set out to write a story about a swing band—and ended up with so much more.

"I feel like I've known both of you so much longer than I have," Trixie said, almost as if she were reading Kit's thoughts. "I can hardly believe everything that's happened in the last few days. What a story!"

"I know," Kit agreed. She hoped that Gibb would think so, too.

Just then, a car came to a sudden stop by the curb just a few yards ahead of Kit and her friends. To Kit's surprise, Gibb stepped out of the car.

"Mr. Gibson!" Kit exclaimed, standing a bit taller.

"Hello, Kit," Gibb said. "I was just on my way home and thought I spotted you. Are these your friends?"

"Yes," Kit said. "This is Stirling, and this is—"

"Trixie," Gibb said, finishing her sentence for her. "Long dark hair and her father's blue eyes—I recognize you from the description in Kit's article."

"You read it already?" Kit asked.

"Sure—I read it as soon as Jimmy put it on my desk. Kit, I must say this is a heck of a story," Gibb said. "As if the concert wasn't enough, Slim seeing his daughter in the crowd, and calling her up onstage ... well, great human interest angle. Readers go for that kind of thing."

Kit's stomach started to flip and flop. "So ... you liked it?" she asked.

"Sure, Kit. But more important, I think our readers will *love* it."

"Does that mean you're going to publish it in the paper? In the grown-up part?" Kit asked.

Gibb couldn't help cracking a smile. "That's exactly what it means."

"Oh, Kit!" Trixie squealed, grabbing Kit to hug her.

Kit hugged Trixie back and then turned to Gibb. She was so breathless with excitement that it took her a moment to find her voice. "I don't know how to thank you," she finally managed to say.

"You don't need to thank me," Gibb said. "You did a very professional job, Kit. One of these days you'll probably be running this newspaper. But for now, that's still my job. Your article will be on the Metropolitan Page of tomorrow's paper."

"Good-bye, Gibb," Kit said. "And thank you!"

Gibb waved over his shoulder and climbed back into his car.

"I can't believe it," Kit said, her eyes shining.

"I can," Trixie said. "You're a great writer. And why not? I've found my long-lost father, and you've got your first major newspaper story!"

"It's crazy!" Kit exclaimed. "It feels like a dream, like everything was moving super slow, and suddenly it's all speeding up."

"Like swing," Trixie said.

Kit looked thoughtfully at Trixie. "It is, isn't it," she said. "And all this happened because I won those tickets from the radio show. What if I hadn't won?"

Trixie smiled. "I think some things are meant to happen," she said. "If they don't happen one way, life finds another way to make them happen if you wish hard enough for them."

"And somehow both our wishes came true," Kit marveled. "All because Swingin' Slim Simpson and his big band came to town. I believe in the magic of swing!"

Inside Kit's World

If Kit's life in the 1930s could have a soundtrack, it would be made up of foot-tapping swing music and soulful jazz. When Kit was growing up, swing could be heard on radios and record players all over America. Swing was so successful because many different types of people could relate to it. Listeners young and old from across the nation were inspired by its upbeat melodies during a difficult time in American history.

In the years of the Great Depression, families unable to afford movie or theater tickets turned to their radios for free entertainment. Kit and Stirling might have enjoyed children's shows like *Terry and the Pirates*, *Dick Tracy*, or the very popular *Little Orphan Annie*. Music programs invited musicians and bands to perform live on the radio, which was a real treat for those who lived in towns where bands' tours never reached.

Jazz and radio had a particularly special relationship. While dance and music venues often separated their white and African American patrons, radio waves didn't discriminate based on the color of the listener's skin. This also made it possible for both black and white jazz musicians to share their music with any listener who tuned in. Before long, bandleaders like Benny Goodman, Louis Armstrong, and Duke Ellington had become household names in black and white communities alike.

As swing music gained popularity on the radio, people made up exciting new dances to go with the lively beat. They flocked to ballrooms and theaters to do the Shag and the Suzy Q, the Big Apple and the Little Peach, and most popular of all, the Lindy Hop. As one music critic put it, "this was a music that was just pure pleasure. Pure physical pleasure."

But while many loved free-spirited jazz for its unpredictable improvisation and swing for its exhilarating energy, others were put off by what they considered to be, simply, "ugly noise." Even Thomas Edison, whose invention of the phonograph made it possible for jazz to be played in households all over the country, claimed that he played jazz records backward because "they sound better that way."

Still others, just like Mr. Steele, were suspicious about this new, wild-sounding music that seemed to encourage such "vulgar" behaviors as close dancing and demonstrations of shameless enthusiasm. In Kit's own Cincinnati, one organization tried to stop the construction of a theater next to a home for expectant mothers, claiming that having jazz performances in close proximity would implant harmful "jazz emotions" in innocent newborn babies! Fortunately, these opinions were shared by a small minority, and jazz continued to lift people's hearts at a time when Americans needed it most.

Jazz remains very popular today, gathering new fans with every broadcast and live performance. Popular jazz festivals take place yearly in most big cities in America as performers, fans, and promoters remain dedicated to keeping the jazz and swing traditions alive for generations to come.

Read more of KIT'S stories,

available from booksellers and at *americangirl.com*

❀ *Classics* ❀

Kit's classic series, now in two volumes:

Volume 1:
Read All About It!
Kit has a nose for news. When the Great Depression hits home, Kit's newsletters begin making a real impact.

Volume 2:
Turning Things Around
With Dad still out of work, Kit wonders if things will ever get better. Could a letter to the newspaper make a difference?

❀ *Journey in Time* ❀

Travel back in time—and spend a day with Kit!

Full Speed Ahead
Help Kit outwit Uncle Hendrick, find a missing puppy, and stay out of jail when she's caught riding a freight train like a hobo! You get to choose your own path through this multiple-ending story.

❀ *Mysteries* ❀

Enjoy more thrilling adventures with BeForever characters.

The Silent Stranger: A Kaya Mystery
Does a strange visitor need help—or will she bring trouble to Kaya's village?

Shadows on Society Hill: An Addy Mystery
Addy's new home holds dangerous secrets—ones that lead straight back to the plantation she escaped from only two years before.

A Growing Suspicion: A Rebecca Mystery
Who is jinxing the Japanese garden where Rebecca volunteers?

The Puzzle of the Paper Daughter: A Julie Mystery
A note written in Chinese leads Julie on a search for a long-lost doll.

❈ *A Sneak Peek at* ❈

Full Speed Ahead

My Journey with Kit

Meet Kit and take an unforgettable journey in a book that lets *you* decide what happens.

B*eep, bee-dle-lee beep beep, beep beep.* It's my phone. My best friend Isabel has just sent me a photo of her pet bunny, Pippa. She is *so cute*!

I call Isabel. "Pippa is adorable," I say. "You are so lucky, Izza! I've asked my mom a million times to let me have a pet."

"And?" Isabel asks.

I sigh, "Sometimes she jokes that my room is so messy a pet would get lost in it. And sometimes she's serious and says that having a pet is a big deal and I'm not responsible enough."

Isabel says, "You were responsible about going to that science day camp thingy this summer—"

"Camp Mosquito!" That's what I called it, anyway. I still have a constellation of bites on my leg in the shape of the Big Dipper.

"You went every day even though you don't especially like creepy-crawlies like bugs or worms."

"Or *sssnakessss*," I hiss.

Isabel giggles. "And I bet you've been responsible

about writing that essay for the first day of school tomorrow, right?"

Uh-oh.

"The *what*?" I gulp. "For *when*?"

"The essay," says Isabel, "due tomorrow."

Terrific. Fifth grade starts tomorrow, and I'm already behind.

Isabel goes on. "You're supposed to write a paragraph about the most important idea you learned this summer."

"Seriously? That's the most boring topic in the world! What did you write about?"

"Pippa," says Isabel, "and how pets teach us about love. Hey! I know what—you could write about Camp Mosquito."

"Mmm-hmm," I say. "How's this?" I put on a deep voice and pretend I'm reading aloud. "The most important idea I learned at science camp is that bug spray isn't repellent but Harry Sharma is. The end."

Isabel giggles mischievously. "You know Harry

only teases you to get your attention, because he has a crush on you."

"Ee-ew!" I protest. "News flash: Harry Sharma is obnoxious and stuck-up and annoying," I tell her, leaving no room for argument. "Listen, Izza, I'd better go. If I start now and write all night long, I *might* get a paragraph written by dawn."

"Okay," Isabel says. "Call me later?"

"Of course," I say. "Bye."

※

I wander into the kitchen to make a snack, thinking about Isabel and how she and her big noisy family are crammed into a teeny house, while I'm an only child rattling around in this humongous super-sleek apartment with my mom—when my mom is here, which she usually isn't. Most of the time, like right now, she's at work. So it's just Sophie the babysitter and me.

I wave to Sophie as I walk through the living

room. She gives me a brief smile but keeps on texting, ignoring me as usual. I think: *If I had a dog, I wouldn't feel so lonely.* Before I turn on the kitchen light, I look out the window. Mom and I live on the top floor of our high-rise, and the walls of our apartment are glass. It's not what you'd call cozy, but I like our apartment at times like right now, when I have a bird's-eye view of the city spread out below me, and lights are twinkling from every building around me. It's as if there's a soft, starry night sky above me *and* below me, and the starry skies meet at the horizon. It gives me a restless, shivery feeling.

I open the refrigerator and see a microwave-safe dish wrapped in plastic with a note from Mom on it:

Heat for 5 minutes.
Early bed. School tomorrow!
Love and kisses, Mom ☺

Haiku, if you don't count the smiley face. I sort of forgot about dinner, and now it's too late to eat it, so I just grab an apple and go back to my room.

My desk is too messy to sit at because I left my grungy softball glove and tennis racket and balls and socks and towels and about a hundred books on it. (I love to read.) I take my laptop and sit on the floor. I type:

The Most Important Idea I Learned This Summer

I stare at that, but I can't think of anything to write except *I wish I had a dog.*

Mom always turns the air-conditioning to sub-zero, so my room is as cold as an iceberg. I grab an old coat out of my project suitcase and snuggle into it. My project suitcase is full of old clothes I'm planning to work on. That's my hobby: going to thrift stores and buying old, vintage clothes. Some of the clothes—like the coat, which I think is from the 1950s—are so cool that I wear them as is. Others I cut apart and reassemble in a totally new way for myself. I know it's a useless kind of hobby, just sort of silly and frivolous. But I don't inflict my creations on anyone, and Mom doesn't seem to mind. She says I'm fearless with the scissors.

In my project suitcase I also find an odd, heavy, rectangular sort of box. It's a camera—a *really* old-fashioned one. It's funky, but cool, with a leather strap. It must have come with a box of clothes; I don't remember buying it. Carefully, I open it up and look down at it into the viewing slot, as if I'm taking a photo. I wonder if it works—does it even have film in it? Slowly, I press the shutter button . . . *click.*

And then,

and then,

and then . . .

I realize it sounds weird and impossible, but the next thing I know, it's broad daylight, I'm in the leafy front yard of a big house, camera still in hand, and a girl who's about my age is walking toward me. And just as weird, right next to me there's a wiggly golden retriever puppy, acting as though he belongs to me and is my best buddy. I pick him up and hold him. If this is a dream, it's a dream come true about the puppy.

"Hi," says the girl, smiling politely.

"Hi," I croak.

"I'm Kit Kittredge," says the girl. "We've been expecting you. You must be Cousin Lucille."

"Lucille?" I repeat. "No." I want to say that I'm not Kit's cousin, and that Lucille is not my name, but I just stammer, "Lu . . . Lu—"

"Oh, okay, I'll call you Lulu if you want," Kit says.

Lulu? Why not? When something's so extreme that it's crazy, don't you call it a lulu? This experience I'm having right now is definitely a lulu.

Kit reaches out and scratches the puppy behind the ears. "Hi there," Kit says to him. She smiles at me, and this time her smile is big and genuine, not stiff and polite like before. "What's your dog's name?"

"He isn't my dog," I tell her. "I don't know who he belongs to."

The puppy licks me on the chin. "He sure seems to think that he belongs to you," Kit says with a grin. "He has no collar or tags. So unless someone claims him, it looks like he's yours if you want him."

"Oh, I do!" I exclaim. "I want a dog more than anything!"

Kit nods. It's clear that she understands completely. "So what are you going to call him?" she asks.

"Buddy," I say. It's the name I've always imagined for my dog, ever since I was little, because that's what I want a dog for—to be my buddy.

"Buddy," says Kit. "That's a cute name. I have a dog named Grace. I love her like crazy. Come on inside and meet her. Everyone will be glad that you're here."

ELIZABETH CODY KIMMEL has written many
books for young adults and teens, including
the Suddenly Supernatural series, *Legend of
the Ghost Dog*, and the Christmas picture book
My Penguin Osbert. Her work has won many
awards, including a Golden Kite Honor Book
Plaque, a School Library Media Specialists'
Rip Van Winkle Award, and the Western Writers
of America Spur Award for juvenile fiction.